ZOMBIESTAN

Read more for young adults from Duckbill

Daddy Come Lately by Rupa Gulab
Facebook Phantom by Suzanne Sangi
Jobless Clueless Reckless by Revathi Suresh
Queen of Ice by Devika Rangachari
Shiva and the Rise of the Shadows by Kanika Dhillon
Skyserpents by Jash Sen
Talking of Muskaan by Himanjali Sankar
The Lies We Tell by Himanjali Sankar
The Right Kind of Dog by Adil Jussawalla
The Wordkeepers by Jash Sen
Zombiestan by Mainak Dhar
When Morning Comes by Arushi Raina
Wanting Mor by Rukhsana Khan
Queen of Earth by Devika Rangachari
Invisible People by Harsh Mander

ZOMBIESTAN

MAINAK DHAR

duckbill

An imprint of Penguin Random House

DUCKBILL BOOKS

USA | Canada | UK | Ireland | Australia
New Zealand | India | South Africa | China | Singapore

Duckbill Books is part of the Penguin Random House group of companies whose addresses can be found at global.penguinrandomhouse.com

Published by Penguin Random House India Pvt. Ltd
4th Floor, Capital Tower 1, MG Road,
Gurugram 122 002, Haryana, India

Penguin Random House India

First published by Duckbill Books

This edition published in Duckbill Books by Penguin Random House India 2020

10 9 8 7 6 5 4 3 2

ISBN 9789381626924

Typeset by PrePSol Enterprises Pvt. Ltd.

Printed at Repro India Limited

www.penguin.co.in

FSC www.fsc.org MIX Paper from responsible sources FSC® C047271

This is a legitimate digitally printed version of the book and therefore might not have certain extra finishing on the cover.

Perhaps fitting that a book about the undead should be dedicated to those who make my life worth living: as always, for Puja and Aaditya.

ONE

Mullah Omar sat down for what would be the last meal of his life.

Of course, at that point he had no way of knowing it would be the last time he'd be eating his frugal repast of dates, bread and figs, but years of living on the run from the Americans had taught him that death could be lurking round any corner. Death was not something that worried him, but the one fear he did have was that he would not be able to see his plans through. The men he was meeting that day were his best, and perhaps his last hope that he might yet live to see the Taliban once again rule over Afghanistan, and the Americans pay for the devastation they had brought upon his people.

Sitting next to Mullah Omar, sharing his meal, was a man who with his thick glasses and flowing white beard looked like a portly college professor. Ayman Al-Zawahiri looked at Omar, sensing the man's apprehension about coming into the open.

'My brother, eat well. After today, we will feast as our enemies burn and rot!'

Omar just shrugged and continued eating.

Al-Zawahiri turned to his own plate. Despite his confident assertion, he had his own fears to contend with. Just months earlier, after Osama bin Laden had been killed,

Al-Zawahiri had been whisked away by his minders in Pakistan's Inter-Services Intelligence from his safe house in Peshawar to a small village on the Pakistan-Afghanistan border. Both Al-Qaeda leaders had been given sanctuary in Pakistan, but after the US's daring raid to kill Osama in the heart of Pakistan, his minders had told him they could no longer guarantee his safety.

Al-Zawahiri had tried to reach out to Al-Qaeda foot soldiers, sure that he could take on the mantle of leadership from Osama. He had been shocked when they paid him no heed. He didn't have the charisma, the vision, or so he heard of them whispering when he was not around. That was why he had hatched this plan, one so audacious that even Osama would never have dreamed of it, and co-opted Mullah Omar, who had come out of hiding in the caves to join him in organising the mission. He knew that without Mullah Omar's help in organising logistics and security inside Afghanistan and Pakistan, his plan would never get off the ground.

The four men with them looked much like Mullah Omar, gaunt and lean from years of living as fugitives in their own land, wearing black turbans that the Taliban favoured, and armed to the teeth. Compared to them, their two visitors looked woefully out of place. They were overweight, dressed in ill-fitting suits and looked exhausted from the journey that had brought them from Pakistan to the small hut nestled on a perch in the Shahikot valley in Afghanistan.

One of them tried to say something, as if anxious to get the business he had come for over with, but Mullah Omar silenced him with a single wave of his hand. He hated being disturbed while eating. It was a habit he had picked up from his mercurial friend. At the thought of his friend, Mullah Omar recalled yet again how the Americans had shot Osama dead in cold blood. He had no great love for the fat Egyptian doctor who fancied himself a revolutionary and thought he could fill Osama's boots, but he was willing to help in a plan that would both avenge Osama's death and bring the Taliban back to power in Afghanistan.

Finally, Al-Zawahiri turned to one of the Pakistanis.

'Now, show me what you've brought.'

The man he had addressed was sweating profusely despite the cold outside; he wiped at his brow with a handkerchief and said, 'We want to serve in the struggle against the infidels. That's why we are here.'

Mullah Omar's eyes narrowed as he studied the man—a soft, city-bred, corrupt government scientist. Intelligence had shown that, in spite all his claims of piety, he spent time with loose women and gambled. Mullah Omar shook his head sadly at what things had come to. Just a few years ago, a sinner such as this would have been stoned to death. Now he not only had to deal with them, but also pay them.

'Hamid, I know all about how pious you are. The five million dollars you want is with us. Now, just show me what you have and let's all get out of here.'

Hamid motioned to his companion, who had been sitting a few feet behind him. The man got up and asked the Taliban bodyguards to help him. Two of the black-turbaned men helped him pull two heavy boxes into the middle of the room.

Mullah Omar studied the boxes curiously. He had never received formal education and the babblings of the scientists meant nothing to him. He knew that science was nothing before the will of Allah. Otherwise, how would a mere village preacher like him have been blessed with the opportunity to lead the faithful in Afghanistan? That conviction had helped him keep his faith even after the infidels had invaded his land and scattered his men.

Hamid started talking, something about Caesium 137 bought from the Chechens, Uranium from Pakistani stocks, Botolinum from Libya and something called Tetrodotoxin.

Mullah Omar felt his head hurting from the complicated words, and stopped Hamid. 'I know nothing of all of this. I just want to know if what you claim this can do for us is true. Abu Jafar, is what these men say true?'

Abu Jafar may have looked like the other Taliban bodyguards, but he was in fact a biotechnology doctorate from an Ivy League university and had worked as a researcher in a leading pharmaceutical company. He had spent the first thirty years of his life as an unremarkable Iraqi immigrant in the US. The wars in Iraq and Afghanistan and the exhortations of the preacher at his local mosque had brought him into the fold, and with his education and qualifications, Osama and Mullah Omar had realised he was meant for greater missions than strapping on a bomb and blowing himself up.

He leaned towards Mullah Omar. 'I have confirmed it. If we use these wisely, we could bring the infidels to their knees.'

Al-Zawahiri, an educated man unlike Omar, was rubbing his hands in satisfaction. Before coming to the meeting, he had done his research on the material these Pakistani scientists claimed to have. He knew that if used correctly, it could devastate the West. The Americans had made such a fuss about weapons of mass destruction, and even destroyed Iraq in their search for some fictional WMDs. Now Al-Zawahiri would show them what mass destruction really meant—when several Western capitals would be hit simultaneously. He smiled at Hamid.

'Then Allah has indeed shown us the way. Give these men their money and see them off.'

Mullah Omar and Al-Zawahiri retreated to the back of the hut while two of the Taliban bodyguards stepped behind the Pakistanis and shot them once each in the back of the head.

'Muzzle flashes! I see muzzle flashes, sir!'

Captain David Bremsak immediately held up his high-powered binoculars to take a closer look at the hut. He could see nothing inside, but he trusted Dan, the sniper in his four-man team. If Dan had seen muzzle flashes inside, then the hut was occupied by someone other than a shepherd. He turned to the bearded man wearing dark wraparound sunglasses to his left.

'Mike, I think we have ourselves something here.'

Mike Fotiou just nodded with a slight smile and picked up his portable radio.

'Eagle Eye, confirm hostile targets at the last coordinates sent.'

There was a click in response.

Mike took off his glasses and looked at David with his

blue eyes. 'You know what I could really do with? A cold beer and some juicy steak.'

David laughed. They had been trekking in the mountains of the Paktia province of Afghanistan for the last fifteen days, living off their rations and the land. They were members of Task Force 121, created to hunt down HVTs, High Value Targets, in the seemingly never-ending 'war on terror'. Osama was dead and fish food by now, but his acolytes were hard at work, and David's job was to hunt them down.

He reached into his pack and took out some chewing gum. 'This is the best I can offer by way of hospitality.'

Mike popped one into his mouth and smiled. The other two men also took the gum that David passed around. Specialist Daniel Barnett had his eyes glued to the scope of his M82A1 Barrett sniper rifle, while Rob Shapiro, to his right had his M4 carbine at his shoulder. The four of them had been inserted into the area when a local informant had passed on news that Mullah Omar, the one-eyed Taliban leader, and Ayman Al-Zawahiri, Osama's deputy, were both reputed to be on the move. In the world of HVTs, that was about as high as it got, and their mission was to report in on movements, and call in air strikes if they found anything.

David saw that Mike had his M4 at the ready by his side. In his two years with TF121, David had worked with a lot of other spooks, but what made Mike better than most CIA desk jockeys who joined them on missions, was the fact that he had been an Army Ranger before joining the CIA's Special Activities Division. He might be a spook now, but he was at heart a warrior like them.

'Holy shit!'

David turned to Dan. 'What the hell did you see? A ghost?'

'Even better, sir. Friggin' Mullah Omar just stepped out to take a leak.'

David stared through his binoculars with incredulity. There was no mistaking the face—he had studied it a dozen times or more in pre-mission briefings. Yes, there he was, Mullah Mohammed Omar, the leader of the Taliban, standing a kilometre away with his pants down, literally. It would have been funny if they did not have some deadly serious business to attend to.

David's orders were clear on what they were expected to do if they did encounter any HVTs. He turned to Dan to tell him to shoot Mullah Omar even as Mike asked Eagle Eye to launch its missiles.

'Dan, take the shot.'

Dan took a deep breath and then fired a single shot. The fifty-calibre bullet fired from the Barrett sniper rifle was designed to punch through light armour. What it did to Mullah Omar's head was not a pretty sight.

The Taliban bodyguards inside saw their leader fall a split second before they heard the unmistakable report of a heavy weapon being fired. They were about to rush out when two Hellfire missiles slammed into the hut, fired by a Predator drone sitting thousands of feet above and a couple of miles away. The explosions incinerated everyone and everything inside.

David had seen more than his share of fighting and killing in his ten years as a Navy SEAL and then with Task Force 121, but this was by far the most exhilarating mission he had ever been a part of. His mind reeled at the implications of what they had achieved. With Mullah Omar gone, it was more than likely that the Taliban would cease to be a unified force, and perhaps be more amenable to a peace deal with the Americans. And if Al-Zawahiri had indeed been with him, then killing him just months after Osama would cripple Al-Qaeda. With this one mission in the mountains of Afghanistan, they may just have changed the course of history.

'Pack up, boys. We don't want to be around when the Taliban get here.'

As silently as they had come, the four men picked up their gear and began their hour-long trek through jagged peaks and narrow passes to reach their exfiltration point, where a chopper was en route to pick them up. They were deep in enemy territory and as much as they would have liked to go in closer to verify their kills, the Predator overhead had already warned them of approaching Taliban forces.

Half an hour after they had left, three pick-up trucks climbed the pass leading to the hut. More than twenty heavily armed, black-turbaned Taliban warriors leapt out, weapons at the ready. But when they saw that they were too late to save their leader, several of them sat down, stunned and in shock.

From the last truck emerged four men dressed in Western clothes. Two of them were white and two black, and they all looked totally out of place. They were Al-Qaeda's most prized foreign operators: men who had been born and brought up in Western society, but had converted to the cause along the way. They had Western identities and passports and could carry their jihad deep into the infidels' lands. They were to have been the carriers of the deadly cocktail of poisons Al-Zawahiri had come to take delivery of.

They stood looking at the burnt remains of the hut and the men who had assembled there. None of them knew the exact contents of the special weapons their leaders had come to take delivery of themselves. Several of the uneducated Taliban warriors poked at the wreckage at random till one of the Western jihadis told them to be more careful. Another wondered aloud if the American Predators were still overhead and if they should just get away as fast as possible.

The Taliban were going to have none of that. They had lost their leaders, and were now collecting body parts, intent on giving Mullah Omar a fitting burial. One or two of the Westerners tried to reason with them that getting away immediately was the only sensible thing to do, but the Taliban soldiers pointed their guns at them and told them to wait. The grisly task of sorting through the charred remains took fifteen minutes—and as they went about it, they inhaled and ingested into their bloodstreams a cocktail of some of the most deadly toxins known to man.

The men were silent, many of them in tears. Their jihad had suffered a massive setback.

Little did they realise that their jihad was going to take on a horrifying new dimension, and that they were to be the ones to strike the first blow in it.

'Mom, I said I'll do it later.'

Mayukh Ghosh put his headphones back on, satisfied that

he had fielded yet another plea by his mother to clean up his room. But this time, it seemed that she was not going to be easily put off. She continued to stand by the door, hands on her hips.

'Young man, you will listen to me when I ask you to do something.'

Mayukh stopped playing on his PS3 and looked up at his mother. When she started any sentence with the words 'young man', it usually meant he was in bigger trouble than usual.

'Mom, it's not a big deal. I'll clean up my room over the weekend.'

Mrs Ghosh moved some of the CDs and sports magazines strewn across his bed and sat down on it.

'This isn't just about your room. You're seventeen now and you'll be in college soon. You need to start thinking more seriously about what you want to do with your life. I mean, look at you.'

Mayukh sighed loudly, which only served to irritate his mother further.

'You just loiter around with that good-for-nothing friend of yours and play video games all day. You need to think about your future.'

Mayukh had already tuned out. He had heard this lecture many times, and was in no mood to hear it again.

'Mom, I know what you're going to say. All your friends' kids are doing well in school, they're so well behaved, they all have a *plan*. I'm sorry I'm such a disappointment, alright?'

With those words, he walked out of his room, slamming the door shut behind him. He knew he would be in big trouble when he got back home, but for now he just wanted to be by himself.

He rode his bicycle for about twenty minutes, the cold November air blasting into his face. Winter was not yet fully upon Delhi, but he was pedalling as fast as he could, and the wind bit into his skin. It was just what he needed to cool down. Finally, his legs aching, he stopped to catch his breath. His long curly hair (another thing which annoyed his mother—why couldn't he get a haircut?) fell all over his face.

What was it about parents, anyways? Whatever he did never seemed to be good enough. And if they had suddenly discovered that he needed to be more responsible, weren't they to blame in any way?

Mayukh's father was a senior government officer. He had grown up surrounded by people ready to do his father's bidding, and had never had to work too hard at anything. For his parents to suddenly wake up and demand that he miraculously become independent was more than a bit unfair, he felt. He was now old enough to realise that his father's connections had got him into the best schools, and ensured that he never had to join a queue to do anything.

He sat at a teashop, drank some Coke and cursed the unfairness of it all. He asked the fat old shopkeeper for a cigarette and the man hesitated, looking at him as if trying to guess how old Mayukh was. At close to six feet and with the physique that came from four years of playing in the school football team, it was impossible to guess he had just turned seventeen. That was till one looked closer at his face—for his eyes were still the open, trusting eyes of a kid. But the shopkeeper was not interested in such subtleties and passed him a Marlboro.

Mayukh puffed away, imagining what his mother would do if she found out he smoked on the sly once in a while. He didn't like it much, and usually coughed his guts out, but none of his friends would ever know that.

His mobile phone beeped. It was his best friend, Shiv. Many things brought the two boys together: a love for cars, distaste for studying, and above all else, a passion for gaming. They could spend hours in front of their PS3s, joining forces in myriad online battlegrounds, blasting away at whatever villains were thrown at them.

'Dude, are we on for our session tomorrow?'

'Of course,' Mayukh replied, and then, remembering the mood his mother had been in, added, 'Hey, is it okay if we meet at your place instead?'

After deciding on a time to meet, they hung up. Mayukh noticed the TV playing in a corner of the shop. There was a banner scrolling across the bottom of the screen.

One or two other people who had come to buy cigarettes at the shop had also stopped to watch. One of them said aloud what was on all their minds.

'That is one screwed-up country, isn't it? First the Taliban, then bloody Osama, then the American war, and now this. They should just nuke it and end the misery.'

Mayukh never spent too much time in front of the TV, least of all watching news, but over the last twenty-four hours, there had been no avoiding the news that had been coming out of Afghanistan. It was all over the Net, and on every news channel. He could hear the newscaster.

'The US military has repeated that the sudden upsurge in violence following the reported deaths of Mullah Omar and Ayam Al-Zawahiri is not a cause for concern but represents the death throes of the Taliban and Al-Qaeda in Afghanistan.'

The screen cut away to a balding, white man in a military uniform.

'We won a major battle in our ongoing war on terror two days ago with the strike that took out the top leadership of the Taliban and Al-Qaeda. The Taliban are now little more than disorganised rabble and the spate of suicide bombings yesterday just show how desperate they are getting in their attempts to destabilise Afghanistan and the progress the democratically elected government has achieved. Our mission is on track and I am confident that the day is not far when peace returns to Afghanistan.'

Mayukh's phone rang again. It was Shiv.

'Dude, what do you want to play—Medal of Honour or Dead Rising?'

Mayukh sniggered. 'Come on, Shiv, don't try and change the game just because I keep wasting you on Medal of Honour.'

There was a pause before Shiv responded. 'But I want to kill some zombies. I was reading this amazing book in which zombies come to life. Wouldn't that be awesome?'

Mayukh took a deep breath. Shiv was cool, but sometimes he took everything too literally. 'Shiv, zombies exist only in frigging video games. Anyway, we're on for tomorrow, and either game, I'm going to whip your ass.'

Abu Jindal, who had once been known as Nadir Dedoune, felt like crap. His head hurt, he kept throwing up every hour or so, and his skin had taken on a strange yellow hue. As he looked at his reflection in the window of the duty-free shop at Karachi airport, he wondered what bug he had picked up.

Perhaps this had all been a stupid idea after all. Growing up as an Algerian immigrant in a poor ghetto outside Paris, he had never known anything other than grinding poverty. There were no jobs, no opportunities, only the condescending and spiteful looks of the rich. That was till he met Mullah Amir, who preached to small groups of young men at the local mosque, and had opened Nadir's eyes to the atrocities being committed against Muslims around the world. He had found a new meaning and purpose to his life—to wage jihad against these infidels. He had made the trip to Afghanistan to take part in some mission that he had supposedly been chosen for. The running around and firing of guns in a camp inside Pakistan had been fun enough, but then he had been totally terrified by what he had seen after the Predator strike that had killed Mullah Omar, Al-Zawahiri and the others. His mission on hold, he had been told to leave immediately.

He bought himself a cup of coffee, but no sooner had he taken a sip than he rushed to the bathroom, emptying the contents of his stomach into the sink. When he had retched himself dry, he washed his face and ran his fingers through his hair. He looked down to see clumps of hair in his hand. In the mirror, he could see a couple of bald patches on his head where the hair seemed to have just come off.

What was happening to him? All he wanted to do now was

to somehow get home and see a doctor. He took out a cap and put it on to cover his head.

'Emirates Flight 605 to Paris via Dubai is now ready for boarding.'

Gratefully, he boarded the flight. It was 5.30 in the morning.

He tried sleeping through the flight, though he had to get up three times during the one-hour flight to Dubai to throw up. On the third occasion he saw blood in the sink.

The flight was delayed in Dubai by several hours, which made him feel even more miserable. A couple of hours after the flight had left Dubai, the woman sitting next to him, bored of watching the sun gradually set over the horizon, turned to order a drink. She saw him start to shake, as if having a fit.

'Sir, are you okay?'

Nadir couldn't hear her. His eyes were glazed over and as he shook even more violently, his cap fell off. He was now nearly bald, his hair lying in clumps all over his seat. As she watched in horror, boils seemed to break out all over his body, oozing pus and blood. He then retched all over the seat in front of him.

Passengers screamed, and a flight attendant called out, asking if there was a doctor on board.

By the time a doctor got to him, Nadir was lying lifeless, a ghastly apparition, covered in his own vomit, pus and blood, a deformed, hairless yellowed being where there had once been a handsome young man.

The French doctor felt for his pulse and then shook his head sadly at the flight attendant.

'Il est mort.'

There were horrified gasps from several of the passengers who had gathered around to see what was happening. The shocked flight attendant turned to her colleague to discuss how they would shift the body, when suddenly, one of the passengers exclaimed, 'Doctor! He's speaking.'

'C'est impossible!'

The doctor leaned over Nadir and saw that his lips were indeed moving. There was still no pulse though. He leaned closer to hear what he was saying. He jerked back when he heard one word.

'Jihad.'

Then Nadir's eyes snapped open.

He sat up calmly, as if nothing had happened, looked around, and grabbed the black scarf from the flight attendant's neck. He proceeded to calmly tie it around his head, as everyone around looked on, speechless.

Then he leapt out to bite the screaming doctor's hand.

On three other flights—headed for New York, London and Washington—the men who had accompanied Nadir to the camp in Afghanistan similarly transformed as the sun set.

David Bremsak was sleeping his first full night's sleep in close to a month. His bunk at Camp Delta just outside the town of Gardez was hardly luxurious, but it beat trudging up and down the Shahikot mountains wondering if he was in some Taliban sniper's sights. He was dreaming of Rose, her long blonde hair, her smell, her touch, when he was woken up. He looked up to see Dan, his M82 in hand.

'Captain, sorry to wake you up.'

David glared at Dan. 'This better be good,' he growled.

Dan reached over and handed David his M4 and vest.

'We're under attack.'

That stopped David's grumbling. He grabbed his gear and rushed out of his cabin. Mike had also just come out of his cabin next door, wearing a Kevlar vest over his T-shirt, and carrying an M4 as well. The CIA officer shouted out at David as he saw him.

'The Taliban must have gone nuts. Trying to attack us here is suicide!'

There were soldiers milling around everywhere. The members of the small TF121 detachment were 'guests' here, sharing the base with its usual occupants, an Army Ranger unit. Given the secretive nature of their HVT hunts, and the time they spent outside in the mountains, David and his men had not really got to know the Rangers too well. But now David saw their Commanding Officer, Major James Lafferty, roaring orders to his men.

'You there, reinforce the western side! I want snipers covering every angle.'

David jogged over to him. Compared to the lean, wiry SEAL, the Ranger Major looked like a giant pit bull.

'What's up?' David asked.

'Two of my boys are down. Some Taliban must have sneaked in and attacked our sentries.'

David considered that for a minute. He had been fast

asleep but there was no way he could have slept through gunfire. James must have read his mind.

'They bit them. We didn't pick them up till they were too close.'

Bit them? David took in the information. 'Did we get them?'

James looked straight at him, and David thought that he saw fear in the big man's eyes.

'The boys pumped them full of bullets, but get this—the two of them fell down, then got back up and ran away.'

'All clear!'

The Ranger who had shouted sounded scared. David could sense that, as word of the raid got around, everyone was spooked. It was one thing to deal with an enemy who shot at you, and reassuringly stayed dead when you shot back. What did you do with enemies who bit you and then got back up when you shot them?

He saw Mike a few feet away. The CIA officer had seen his share of crazy stuff, but this was too weird even for him.

'Do you reckon there's any truth to this at all?'

'Mike, I've seen all kinds of terrorists and tough guys. They all like to talk it up, but believe me, when you shoot them, they all stay down. Our boys must have just panicked. Most of them are kids on their first combat tour. I bet they didn't hit those Taliban once.'

The Rangers were now busy tending to the two wounded men, who were bleeding profusely from bites to their hands and necks.

'Get them Medevaced now!'

The following morning, the injured men were airlifted

to Kabul. They were put on a flight to Ramstein airbase in Germany when doctors at the base in Kabul said they could not deal with the strange symptoms they were seeing.

When the flights landed in Germany, horrified medics found everyone on board bitten and scratched by their patients.

David and his team were out on the road again. He had heard that he was being recommended for a Navy Cross for the mission that had taken out Mullah Omar and Al-Zawahiri. Medals were always nice, but the biggest thing on his mind was the fact that he was finally doing something that mattered. His father, a New York fire fighter, had perished in the rubble of the World Trade Center, and David had dedicated every single moment of his life since that day to avenging his father and the thousands of others who had died on 9/11. He didn't look like much a warrior, at five feet eight, with a lean body, but what he lacked in size, he more than made up in determination and speed. He had hung in there when stronger and more experienced men had quit all around him at SEAL training in Coronado, and then he had taken his revenge in missions around the world, from Iraq to Afghanistan.

And now, his team's mission was to find the 'undead'. Over the last couple of days, rumours had spread like wildfire all over Afghanistan. Tales of black-turbaned Taliban who had come back from the dead, and who could not be killed. Monsters who had superhuman strength and speed, and were rampaging through whole villages at night, biting and scratching people, and then disappearing into the mountains.

David and his team were to check out the last reported sighting. Their brief was simple. Find out if these mythical 'undead' Taliban existed, and if they did, shoot a few of them dead to prove to the Afghan people that they were just a figment of someone's imagination, or as David suspected, the Taliban propaganda machine in overdrive.

They were an hour into their hike through the hills when Rob spotted some movement behind them in the dark. David turned around to see a black turbaned man standing on a small hillock just fifty feet behind them.

How the hell had anyone got on their tail without their noticing it?

David brought his M4's scope to his eyes. With his night vision optics on, what he saw was bathed in a ghostly green light. Their stalker had a black turban tied around his head in the fashion the Taliban favoured, but the rest of him scarcely looked human. Despite the cold, he was wearing tattered clothes, revealing a body covered in boils, pus and blood. His skin was a sickly yellow and his mouth was open, revealing teeth with jagged, sharp edges.

'Dan, drop the bastard!'

Dan brought up his M82 to his shoulder, but even before he could take aim, the man had disappeared from sight, moving faster than David had seen any man move.

Just then Rob screamed an ugly, keening sound.

David turned to see him on the ground, a black-turbaned man on his chest, leaning over and biting his shoulders and chest. David's M4 was up in a flash and he fired a three-round burst into the man. The shots sent the man sprawling against the rock face, but then to David's horror, the man got up.

Close up, he looked even more horrible than the other man David had seen through his scope. He smelt like a cross between a dead mouse and a toilet that had not been flushed or cleaned for some time. His eyes were focused on David, and his lips were drawn back, revealing sharp, blood-covered teeth.

He leapt at Mike with surprising speed and bit him in the arm. The CIA officer had his handgun out and fired three 9mm rounds at point-blank range even as the man's teeth sank into his left hand. The black-turbaned man fell to the ground, and then seemingly jumped off the edge. David peered over to see him climbing down the sheer rock face.

He looked back at the two men on the ground, blood oozing from their wounds. David had never been a particularly religious man, but he crossed himself, shuddering at the horror of what he had just seen with his own eyes.

TWO

Hina Rahman stood up to get a cup of coffee, her creaking joints reminding her that she had come a long way from the days when she had been the heartthrob of every boy in college. Now she was the crotchety old professor who nagged them to do their assignments. Nobody would have told her that to her face, but while her joints may have weakened with age, her hearing was still good.

As she savoured the hot drink, she turned on the TV. Every news channel seemed to have only one thing to report, the so-called Afghan Flu. She left CNN on as she set the dinner table. Over the clinking of glasses, plates and cutlery, she heard the sombre voice of the newscaster.

'In less than three days since its first appearance, what doctors are calling the Afghan Flu is spreading like wildfire. Medical authorities are saying that there is still no cause for panic, but have warned against any travel to Afghanistan or Pakistan.'

Hina sniggered to herself. There wasn't exactly a long queue of tourists waiting to brave roadside bombs and drone attacks in India's two dysfunctional Islamic neighbours! Her father, a devout Muslim born in Lahore, would have probably hit her for such thoughts, but her home was Delhi, not Pakistan, which she had left at the age of one during the Partition in 1947. And while she considered herself a devout

Muslim too, she found nothing in common with the hateful radicals who seemed to hold sway nowadays in Afghanistan and Pakistan.

She put the last plate in its place and then turned to the TV. She flipped the channel to BBC, where they were interviewing the American president, who was in London for a summit. She had welcomed his election, one of the reasons being she found him strikingly handsome. Sixty-five summers had not robbed her of the emotions and sense of humour that had once made her a vivacious young woman.

His eyes seemed filled with trepidation as the president spoke.

'Ladies and gentlemen, we have been through a number of outbreaks before—swine flu, bird flu, SARS, and many others. My heart goes out to everyone affected by this latest outbreak and their families, but I do want to reassure all of you that medical science is now at such a level that we can contain and eventually turn back such outbreaks.'

One of the reporters asked, 'Mr President, could you update us on the latest number of confirmed cases in the US and Great Britain?'

The president turned to ask one of his advisors and, for a brief moment shook his head as if in disbelief. Then he responded.

'We now have four thousand people in quarantine in the United States and two thousand here in England. Total confirmed cases worldwide stand at just under fifteen thousand.'

There was a collective gasp from the gathered reporters.

Hina found herself mumbling a prayer. Fifteen thousand

in just over two days? What disease was this that turned people so crazed that they bit anyone who came near them, and one bite was enough to infect a victim? And what about those rumours about them dying and coming back to life? How did medical science explain that?

Before the reporters could ask any more questions, the president had left.

Hina changed the channel to NDTV India, which was reporting the first confirmed cases in India. One of the 'experts' was responding to a question on how the disease could have spread so fast.

'As far as we know, the infection was first spotted in a few young men flying out of Afghanistan through Pakistan. Hence the name. Then there are the American soldiers who developed the symptoms while being flown to Germany and infected dozens of others. Consider this simple fact: there are an estimated four million people travelling by air every single day across the world. Add people meeting them at airports, their families, staff on the planes and at airports, the taxi drivers who ferry them and so on. Literally each traveller could be in close contact with hundreds of people every day. So it's not surprising that the number of infections outside of Afghanistan and Pakistan has exploded so fast.'

Hina turned off the TV. It was a depressing enough day without having to worry about an exotic virus and its bizarre effects.

She finished her coffee and brought the small cake she had baked to the table. She sat in the same chair where she had sat for meals for the last thirty years. To her right was the head of the table, where Imran once sat. She stifled a sob at the memory. No, today was a day for celebration, not for sorrow.

She blew out the candle and cut a big slice that she placed on a plate. She put it at Imran's place, where he would have once wolfed it down in a few bites. She took a small slice herself and whispered, 'Happy birthday, darling.'

That night, as for more than a dozen years, Hina ate alone. As usual, the table had been set for four. One for Imran, the love of her life, who had been taken from her by a heart attack; and two for her children, now in distant America, with lives and families of their own. Arranging plates for them served to remind her of a family that had once been, and yes, it also made her feel less lonely.

She finished eating and then booted up her MacBook Air. She may have been sixty-five, but when it came to technology, she was not a second behind any of her students. She surfed the Net for some time, and tiring of reading more gloom and doom about the Afghan Flu, she began to write.

This was the time of day when Hina felt all her worries lifting. When it was just her and her imagination, and of course her trusty keyboard, over which her fingers were now flying, almost as fast as the ideas coursing through her head. This was also her little secret. Hina Rahman, erudite history professor by day, was also Alice Flowers, the author of a number of internationally bestselling historical romances, much praised for the lyrical writing and historical authenticity, but occasionally criticised for their graphic nature. Alice had been the name of her favourite school teacher who had first encouraged her to write; and Flowers was the literal translation of her Urdu name.

Tonight, her mind was not really on her writing. She kept thinking of Rumana, her daughter in Boston, and Said, her son in New York. With the infection spreading so fast, she hoped they and their families were okay. She decided to call them to check. She was not able to get through; all the networks seemed congested.

She checked CNN.com. There was a lot of breaking news and none of it was good.

'Doctors say fatal levels of radiation and toxins found in blood of infection victims.'

'Fifty thousand infected worldwide.'

And then she saw a line scrolling across the bottom of the screen that sent a shiver down her spine.

'All contact with Kabul and Peshawar lost. Last reports speak of hordes of Afghan Flu victims going on a rampage as the sun set.'

Her children would not answer their phones, and she finally went to bed, as she had an early lecture the following morning.

Sleep eluded her. All night, she heard the sounds of police and ambulance sirens outside.

Could it really have spread to Delhi so fast?

At six in the morning, she gave up all attempts to sleep and turned on the TV.

The night had been of a kind that Asia had never seen before. As soon as the sun set, hundreds of infected people across the continent had seemingly died and then come alive and attacked anyone in sight. The number of new patients was in the tens of thousands. Some of the original attackers had been caught and quarantined, but the vast majority had slipped away at daybreak, not to be seen again. Thousands of victims were in hospital, but with no apparent cure, the authorities at a total loss as to what to do with them. If the cycle started at sunset, as many were now guessing, she wondered what the next night would bring.

A thought struck her. The sun was just setting in the United States. She turned to CNN and watched the images in horror. Whole cities were burning, and the streets were full of infected people on the rampage. Through the camera of a helicopter, she got her first look at them, and her blood froze. It was a large mob, moving with a stiff gait, and as the camera zoomed in, she saw that they were yellowed and covered in filth and blood. For some inexplicable reason, they all wore black turbans. And then, they ran at a dizzying speed, more like a pack of animals than men, at a group of people huddled inside a 7-Eleven store. The camera mercifully panned away as they reached their victims.

BBC showed similar images from other parts of the world. The reporters looked too frightened to really be credible bearers of news. She was sure of that when a young BBC reporter said that the government had called the army onto the streets, but soldiers had told her that their bullets had no effect on the mobs. The reporter said, eyes wide in horror, that after taking several bullets, the infected would just get up and resume their crazed attacks.

Hina was sure that the reporters must have got some of their facts mixed up.

Then the channels started going off the air.

At the breakfast table, Mayukh saw an emotion he had never seen before on his father's face: fear. A career bureaucrat in the home ministry, which he had joined as a member of the Indian Police Service, the elder Ghosh was used to wielding power and influence, not feeling helpless. Yet, this morning, he listlessly stirred his bowl of cereal, bloodshot eyes staring at the TV set.

'Dad, are you unwell or something?'

Mayukh had spent the evening playing World of Warcraft online and listening to music. He had no idea of the chaos that was slowly but surely intruding upon his world.

His son's presence made Ghosh try to compose himself. 'No, Mayukh, I just didn't sleep much. I was on the phone almost the entire night.'

Mayukh knew his father had a busy job, but even by his standards, it was unusual to be up all night working. His mother entered the room. She also looked as if she was on the verge of a breakdown.

That's when he noticed the Breaking News scrolling across the TV screen. He watched in silence for about five minutes, taking in what was supposedly happening around the world. He saw the pictures and heard the words, but his mind refused to believe it. He turned to his father, seeking reassurance.

'Dad, most of the Indian news channels are full of crap anyway. Let's turn on CNN or something.'

Before his father could say anything, Mayukh had flipped the channel to CNN, and then BBC. Both channels were off air, and instead of the usual programming, there was a multi-coloured screen across which was written three words: 'Emergency Broadcast System'.

Mayukh's father took the remote control from him.

'All the western channels have been off air since last night. We know the US president is safe—he managed to fly out on Air Force One and is currently at a secure base somewhere—but have no idea what's happened to the rest of their governments. Nobody is responding to our questions.'

Mayukh looked at his father blankly. Stuff like this only happened in the movies, didn't it? Surely there was a misunderstanding somewhere. He began to sputter out some objection when his father silenced him.

'Mayukh, listen to me. I have to go to work. Whatever has taken the West will be upon us as soon as the sun sets.'

Mayukh's mother broke into quiet sobs.

'But Dad, why can't you just stay with us?'

His father gripped Mayukh's shoulders and forced him to look into his eyes.

'You're not listening. If the US and Britain have fallen, we don't have much of a chance. Still, I have a responsibility to fulfil. If our government just folds up and runs, who will try and maintain some order?'

His mother was crying uncontrollably.

His father continued. 'Mayukh, I know this is going to be tough for you, but this is the day when you need to stop being a boy and become a man. I will be gone, and I don't know when I will see you again, but you need to hold it together for yourself and your mother. Now come with me.'

He led Mayukh to his study. Mayukh was petrified and on the verge of tears.

His father opened a safe in the wall and took out a small bag from it. Mayukh knew what was in it, and that recognition only made him more afraid. He could feel his heart pounding and his mouth seemed to have suddenly gone dry as his father approached him. He had often fantasised about being given free access to what was in the bag, but now that it was being handed to him, he wished it had never come to this. His father took out the one item it contained and placed it in Mayukh's palm. It was his father's personal licensed weapon.

Mayukh could see that his father's eyes seemed to be tearing up, but that he was trying to be strong so his son would not lose courage. Somewhere Mayukh knew that his life was about to change forever, and he let his tears fall.

His father's voice was soft, like it used to be when he read stories to Mayukh years ago.

'Son, what is this? Tell me. I need to hear you say it. Tell me everything you know about it.'

'It's a Smith & Wesson Bodyguard 380. Weight 335 grams, holds 7 rounds in its clip. And I can still outshoot you on the range.'

His father smiled, and held Mayukh close. He realised his son was trying in turn to give him courage. They sat together for some time, hands in each other's and on the small black handgun.

Mayukh's father had been a national-level shooter in his youth. Being in the police, he had continued to have ample opportunity to indulge in his love for shooting. That was one passion he and Mayukh shared. Mayukh had been a natural shooter, with instincts that could never have been taught, but he'd never had the discipline to compete, much to his father's disappointment. Now, however, he was just grateful his father had taught him how to shoot. Then, something struck him.

'Dad, my carrying this weapon is illegal, isn't it? And you being a cop and all, won't you get into trouble?'

His father gave him a tired smile. 'I suspect that will be the least of our worries. Remember, keep it well hidden, and while I have four full clips and enough rounds for ten refills, don't fire unless you or your mother are in immediate danger. Understand?

'I have to go now, son. Be the man I always dreamed you would be.'

His father left.

A few minutes later, Mayukh's mother walked in, and for all the times he had fought with her, been irritated and hated her for disciplining him, now he just hugged her close and cried like a baby.

After they had seemingly cried themselves dry, his mother took charge. Mayukh had never seen her like this, and her determination and clarity of thinking galvanised him into action.

'Mayukh, we need to stock up on food. God knows how long this will go on, so we need to be ready. Take the car and get as much canned food and bottled water as you can find. Go now while I prepare the house.'

Mayukh had pleaded with his parents in vain for months

to be given a chance to drive their Honda City. Now, the keys were being literally handed to him.

As he drove out of their government colony, he began to see that they were not the only ones preparing for what was to come. Many of the stores were packed with people, and here and there, frayed tempers had led to fights. Not fancying his chances at these shops, he drove to his usual teashop where he bought cigarettes.

The fat old shopkeeper, whose name he had never asked, had his radio held close to his ears. He looked up at Mayukh. 'Take what you want and go. Better an old customer than being looted by strangers.'

Mayukh didn't understand what he was talking about at first, but then saw smoke rising from some of the neighbouring stores. He passed over a thick wad of cash to the disbelieving man. The small teashop didn't have much by way of canned food, but had lots of chips, cookies, juices and bottled water—all of which would last a long while. Mayukh took as much as he could fit in the boot of his car and then drove back home.

He was about to enter the colony when the windshield shattered, showering him with glass fragments. He flinched and almost crashed the car, recovering just in time to steer the car through the gate. He could see several people outside, no doubt envious at the relative security the government colony with its guards and high gates would provide. He wondered if any of that would be enough to weather the approaching storm.

David clutched his rifle and held his breath, aware that his hunters would give him no quarter if they got the slightest hint that he had got away. He could hear moaning and screaming all around him, and above all else, the shuffling noises of the hunters on the prowl. He tried to shake the idea out of his mind that two of them had till a few hours ago been men he would have trusted his life with. He closed his eyes, shrinking further behind the ammunition boxes where he had wedged himself. He thought of Rose, to whom he had proposed just before this deployment. All he wanted was to get back to her.

It had all started as soon as the sun had set.

After the attack in the hills, David had taken Mike and Rob back to camp. With both of them in excruciating pain, it had taken them four hours to get back, and David had been horrified at the changes the two men had undergone during that time. Both lost hair, bled from open sores, and their skin began to turn yellow. All day, the medics had worked on them, but their condition seemed to get worse, till the horrific transformation that set in at sunset.

At least five other victims of similar attacks came in from patrols across the province. The medics had been unable to do much for them, and the Ranger Commander had already decided that they would be flown out the following morning.

David had been in his cabin in the evening when he was told that Mike was asking for him. It had been just before sunset, and when he reached him, the once rugged CIA officer was looking like a ghost of his former self. His teeth seemed crooked and his skin was completely yellow. The sores on his body gave off a terrible stench, as did the vomit that covered the floor. David had seen a lot of blood and killing, but he had never seen anything like this before. The young medic attending to Mike was shaking.

Mike seemed to want him to come closer so he could say something, but suddenly his back arched and he screamed as if he were in extreme pain. Two medics tried to hold him down in vain, and then, as suddenly as he had screamed, he fell back limply on the bed. David watched as the medics turned to him sadly and told him Mike was no more. David stumbled out of the cabin, dazed by what he had seen when he bumped into another medic who told him that all seven men who had been infected were dead.

Then the horror began.

SEAL operative though he was, nothing had prepared David for what followed. There was the constant din of guns firing, and of soldiers screaming as the seven men tore into those who had been their colleagues and buddies. Initially unable to fire on those who had been friends, David had finally unloaded a full magazine into one of the rampaging Rangers, but then realised what all the other soldiers at the base were finding out. The creatures that their friends had transformed into could not be killed by bullets.

Then David did what he had to do to survive. He hid as the frenzied attack continued all around him. A bizarre detail David remembered was that in the midst of all the carnage, the infected men had stopped when they could to tie crude black turbans around their heads.

The sliver of gold on the ground next to him grew into a broad band of light. The shouting and yelling was replaced by the quieter sounds of wounded men. As the sun rose, the attacks stopped.

He stepped out from his cover and saw a scene straight out of hell. Wounded American soldiers littered the base, bleeding from bites on their bodies. One or two who had presumably tried to fight back the hardest were dead. One of them was the Ranger Commander. The man had dwarfed all the other men at the base, but he was now lying on the ground, his neck snapped, his body limp like a rag doll.

David leaned against a wall for support when he saw Dan lying on the ground, bleeding from several bites. His old team member was looking at him, pleading for help. But after what he had just seen, David knew there was nothing he could do to help him.

He entered the communications room and tried to radio for help—and then realised that their base was not the only one to be hit. Bases across Afghanistan had been attacked, and there were reports of mobs of infected people attacking thousands of victims in Kabul and other cities. Wounded men on board US navy ships off Pakistan had also gone on a rampage, infecting dozens. He could hear someone on the radio, stammering in fear and confusion.

'Man, it was like being in a zombie movie.'

He wasn't going to get any help; all the survivors were too shell-shocked and had enough problems of their own. He sent in a situation report, asking for medics to come in and care for the wounded men at the base. That was when he got a sliver of hope. Someone from on board the *USS Kearsage*, the command ship for the special operations forces in Afghanistan, spoke up.

'Soldier, everyone's in a world of pain, and I don't know how much we can do for you, but we are sending choppers out to get folks like you to safety in Pakistan. Be at this place by sunset,' he said, and gave David the coordinates.

It was a twenty-mile hike, and David knew he could make it there by sunset. Not knowing what to expect along the way, he took his time preparing. He stuffed his pack with MREs. Many new soldiers hated the Meals Ready to Eat packs, but David had learnt, if not to like them, to accept them. He took as many extra clips for his M4 assault rifle as he could, and then he set out for his journey to the extraction point.

At the best of times, the landscape was bleak in this part of Afghanistan. What made it infinitely worse now was the presence of several injured and bleeding people lying on the roads. Clearly the American bases had not been the only places attacked the previous night, and David shuddered as he wondered what was to come when the sun set again. The Americans could at least try to quarantine the injured soldiers, but for these villagers, there was nothing to be done.

What was eerie was the total absence of the infected people who had gone on a rampage the previous night. They had seemingly disappeared, though more than once David got a feeling that hidden eyes were watching him. Once, while passing through an abandoned village, he took out his M4 and was about to go into a hut where he was sure someone was watching him. But then, remembering the events of the previous night, he decided discretion was the better part of valour and continued on his journey.

Even with the weight he was carrying, he reached the

extraction zone by four in the evening. He radioed his position and then sat on a nearby perch, his weapon at the ready.

At five, a pick-up truck rumbled into view. David's senses went into overdrive. The black-turbaned men riding at the back, carrying AK-47s and RPGs, could be nothing other than Taliban warriors on patrol. There must have been at least six of them, and David knew that, out in the open as he was, he was a sitting duck.

He was not going to go down without a fight. In less than a second, he had his gun's safety off and the M4 was tracking the cab of the truck.

He was about to pull the trigger when the truck stopped less than fifty metres away, and he saw that the Taliban were making no move to attack him. One of them got down and looked at him. David put his rifle down when he realised that the men were not about to attack him. If anything, they looked terrified. The man looking at him simply pointed to the sun and then they were on their way.

They were doing exactly what he was planning—trying to get to safety before the sun set.

About fifteen minutes later, he heard a buzzing sound and looked up to see an OV-22 Osprey come into view. The tilt rotor craft could take off and land vertically like a helicopter, and then fly in level flight like an aircraft. The Osprey landed just a few metres away. David sprinted to it, feeling a huge wave of relief wash over him as he entered it. There was only one soldier inside the craft.

'Sergeant, didn't you get anybody else?'

The man looked at David, a haunted look in his eyes.

'None of the others were clean.'

The full extent of the catastrophe hit David. He asked why he was not being flown to the *USS Kearsage*. The soldier turned away before answering.

'Sir, ten infected men are on board. Last I heard the skipper was debating whether to kill them before sunset. They have already authorised cruise missile strikes on bases where only infected men are left.'

David braced himself as the craft took off, wondering if things had indeed gotten so bad that they were considering killing their own soldiers. The rest of the ride passed in total silence till they reached the Shamsi airbase in southern Pakistan.

David had never been there, but he knew it was the major staging ground for the US drone effort over Afghanistan. He could see soldiers milling around as other choppers and Ospreys landed, bringing in evacuees like him. Many of the men and women around him looked terrified. He wondered if he looked any different.

Shamsi had once been a private airbase where rich Arab sheikhs came to practise falconry. Over the last few years, it had been transformed into a state-of-the-art facility from which hundreds of Predator strikes had been launched. Officially, the base did not exist.

David was still standing near the flight line when a sudden silence descended upon the base. His eyes were drawn up, in the direction everyone else was looking at.

The sun had just begun to set.

A soldier came up next to him, talking to nobody in particular.

'They say the base is clean, but who knows what's out there?'

Another soldier spoke up.

'We've got five Ospreys with Gatling guns and fixed base defences that could stop a battalion. I don't think we need to worry.'

Having been through what he had in the last two days, David was not so sure about that. How did you keep out attackers you could not kill?

Nothing seemed to happen for some time, but the soldiers were so much on edge, they refused to take their backpacks off. Most wandered about, carrying loaded weapons, waiting for what would be coming at them over the walls.

When the attack began, it was as unexpected as it was vicious. David, like everyone else, had expected the zombie-like creatures to try and come in on foot. Instead, a huge truck came rolling towards the base's main gate, pushed by a horde behind it. The machine-gun fire bounced off it, and it stopped just short of the gate where three anti-tank missiles hit it.

As the truck exploded, David could hear no cheering. Everyone at the base had just had a terrifying realisation: the infected were not just mindless zombies; they were learning, adapting, even trying crude tactics. And it had just been a few days since it had begun.

A commotion at the rear of the base had soldiers scrambling there. He heard someone screaming, 'There's got to be at least a thousand of them coming!'

David scrambled up a watchtower to get a better look, unslinging his rifle as he climbed.

As far as the eye could see, there were infected men and women trying to enter the base. Soldiers unloaded bullets into the hordes as fast as they could, but the infected would only fall and then get back up. Several got tangled in the barbed-wire fence, but the others climbed over them.

David took aim and squeezed one round, seeing one attacker fall. To his surprise, this one didn't get back up. Did shots to the head kill them? Did all those zombie movies actually get that one right?

A minute later, his hopes were dashed. The man, if that was what the creature could be considered anymore, got up and rejoined his friends in storming the base. Head shots didn't kill, but it did put them down for some time. David wondered if he'd stay alive long enough to put that knowledge to any use. The thought that he could turn into a mindless creature like those milling around in front of him was too horrible to even contemplate.

As the attackers began swarming through the base, David saw some soldiers turn their weapons on themselves, preferring to die instead of being turned into the monsters that now teemed around them. David considered the idea, but then Rose's face came before his eyes. He had to live. He had to get out.

One of the Ospreys had its rotors on, a young pilot standing nearby, too terrified to do anything. David ran to him.

'Son, can you fly this?'

The pilot nodded.

'Then let's get out of here!'

The man just looked at him blankly.

'But I haven't got my flight orders yet.'

David realised he was in shock. He grabbed him by the shoulders hard and shook him.

'Kid, see those monsters coming? They'll rip your neck out in a second. Let's get out while we can.'

He climbed into the Osprey's cockpit as the pilot prepared for take-off. The base was now teeming with the infected, and David could see fallen soldiers everywhere. He now also knew that the next day, as soon as the sun set, these soldiers would join the hordes who had attacked them. As they flew by, the roads filled with mobs of the infected, moving in their slightly stiff gait.

He looked straight ahead, and felt something wet on his face. He checked to see if he was bleeding, and saw that without realising it, he had been crying.

'Kid, where do we go?'

The pilot now seemed to be more in control, but his hands still shook as he checked the map.

'Sir, I'd go to India. It may not have spread there so fast.'

After a few minutes, David asked him which city they were flying over. The pilot looked at him with tired eyes.

'Does it matter?' he said. 'It's all Zombiestan down there.'

THREE

HINA SAW that the sun was about to set and drew the curtains. She had gone to college in the morning but had found it deserted. The principal, who lived just off the campus, had looked at her as if she were out of her mind.

'Ms Rahman, I would go home and be with my family, if I were you.'

And so she had come home. She knew that if her family had still been with her, she would have reacted very differently. She could understand why her colleagues were in a state of panic: they were terrified about losing people or things precious to them in the chaos that threatened to engulf them when the sun set.

Hina had nothing to lose. And certainly she had nowhere else to run to. She had lived in this two-storeyed colonial house for the last thirty years, and could not imagine going anywhere else. Her children were still not picking up their phones, and while she hoped that they were fine, even when things had been normal, they had often been too busy to take calls from their forgotten old mother back home.

She sat down at her desk in the study on the first floor. The shelf in front of it was lined with books, and as she booted up the laptop, she wondered when people would read books again. Would there be a time in the future when books would be written about the period when humanity had gone crazy under the influence of some mysterious plague and nearly destroyed itself? She hoped so. It would be awful if nobody read books again.

She began typing, but found that she just could not concentrate with the sounds of panic coming from outside: of people trying to get home, pressing on their car horns, people shouting at others to get out of their way.

As soon as the sun set, an ominous silence descended, as if some giant unseen hand had just pressed the mute button on the world. Hina peeked out through the curtains and saw that everyone unfortunate enough to still be outside had stopped to look at the setting sun.

Then it began.

The first sign of the chaos that was to come was the sound of guns being fired. There was a police station nearby and she figured the cops were trying to keep things under control. Then she heard screaming, and then the guns stopped firing.

Hina turned off the lights in her study. She had opened a new bottle of wine and now finished her glass in a long swallow, her heart hammering as she wondered what would come next.

People on the road were running now, and several were screaming. There were desperate cries for help outside her home, and Hina wanted to do something to help. But what could a frail old woman possibly do?

Hina looked down from her first-floor window to the road below to witness a scene that would forever be etched in her mind. There was a mob of people—no, creatures would be a more accurate description—transformed by the infection to mindless wild animals. They all seemed to be wearing black turbans, men and women alike, and with their tattered clothes, yellow skin and bloodied bodies, looked nothing like the people they must have been just a day ago. They wandered through the street in their stiff gait and every time they saw anyone, they would attack like a pack of wild animals, surrounding their prey and scratching and biting till they brought them down. Hina saw one or two young men try and fight back, and she watched in horror as they were killed, their necks broken by their crazed attackers.

She watched a young girl, perhaps no more than fifteen, running from one house to another, pleading with the occupants to let her in, to give her some refuge. But there was no safety anywhere today.

The creatures had entered several homes along the road and the screams coming from inside them told Hina what the fate of their occupants—her long-time neighbours—would have been.

The young girl was now directly below Hina's window. Despite the darkness inside, she saw Hina peeking out from behind the curtains.

'Please let me in. Please help me.'

Hina looked straight into the girl's eyes and then saw four of the creatures moving towards her.

She could have gone down and let the girl in, but then the creatures would no doubt see her and force their way into the house. She stayed rooted where she was, paralysed by fear, as the girl tried to run, only to be encircled and then brought down by her attackers.

Crying at her weakness and ashamed at having done nothing to help, Hina hid under her desk, praying that they would think there was nobody home.

An eternity later, but what was perhaps just five minutes, when the sounds of the attack outside abated, Hina worked up the courage to part the curtains and look down.

The girl was lying there, curled in foetal position, blood all around her. Suddenly, spasms seemed to go through her body, and then, after a violent jerk, she lay still again. Then the girl suddenly sat upright and looked at Hina. Her face was yellowed and bloodied, and her eyes narrowed in hate. She scrambled around, as if looking for something, and then tore off a portion of her black skirt which she tied around her head.

Hina's heart was pounding. Everyone had said that the infection took one day to transform its victims. It seemed that the effects were now taking hold of their victims in ten minutes or less, transforming healthy, decent people into bloodthirsty, crazed killers. No wonder so many countries had gone under so fast.

The girl pointed straight at Hina and emitted a shrill, ear-piercing scream. Several of the other creatures started to come towards her. Hina knew that she was trapped, with no way out.

Less than two kilometres away, Mrs Ghosh was struggling to start the car. The keys dropped from her shaking hands for the third time.

Mayukh saw that his mother was on the verge of a breakdown, and took hold of her hand.

'Mom, let me drive.'

She handed over the keys without any protest.

His mother had believed that they would be safe in their government colony, with the armed guards who usually were on duty outside. However, by evening, it was clear that she had been badly mistaken. When Mayukh had gone out at about four to see what was happening outside, he saw that all but one of the guards had left their posts.

The remaining man had shrugged and said, 'They all have families. I can't blame them for wanting to get home before sunset.'

The TV channels had reported that as the sun slowly set over Asia, the darkness took hold over one country after another. The pattern was the same. As soon as the last light faded, those who had been infected transformed into bloodthirsty creatures, ravaging anyone in sight.

His father had called earlier in the day saying that if their colony did not appear safe, then they were to try and get to the old Kotla stadium, which was being heavily fortified as a safe haven. Mrs Ghosh had waited till the last moment, perhaps too long, to decide that they were better off trying to reach the stadium instead of staying at home.

The sun was about to set.

Mayukh started the car and they left the colony. They had packed their car with as many provisions as they could, and Mayukh had the loaded handgun next to him.

He turned to look at his mother. She was looking to him to lead the way. Seeing his mother so vulnerable scared him more than anything else, reminding him that things were well and truly out of control now.

Mayukh was jolted back to reality by the repeated staccato sound of guns firing nearby.

'Mom, the firing seems to be coming from the police station. We can't go that way. Let's try and find another route.'

She just nodded.

He knew another way to Kotla, but it meant he had to drive through a narrow road, crammed with houses and several alleys leading off on either side.

Concentrating on trying to identify the right turn, Mayukh never saw the three men who ran into their car. His mother screamed as the window on her side shattered and a yellow, bloodied arm reached in.

Mayukh slammed his foot on the accelerator and their attackers were left behind as their car shot ahead.

Another infected man came right in front of his car. Mayukh made the mistake of trying to swerve out of the way. The car hit a small shop on the sidewalk and his head hit the steering wheel with a sickening thud. Blinded by pain, he could hear his mother shouting.

'Hurry up! They're coming!'

Mayukh reversed the car, feeling the impact as he hit someone or something, and then raced down the road. There were now people running all over the street, many of them pursued by shrieking attackers.

A group of five infected men emerged from the shadows to their left. Mayukh steered the car into a gut-wrenching turn and sped into one of the alleys to his right. He raced out from the alley onto the main road, where just a hundred metres to the right, attackers were beginning to break down the front door of Hina Rahman's house.

David came out of the Osprey, his rifle at the ready. In the fading light, he tried to make out if anyone was there at the airfield. It seemed deserted. On their way in, the young pilot had tried to make contact with the Indian Air Force base at Hindon, just outside Delhi, and also the international airport. Both had been closed to all traffic, in anticipation of the chaos that was to unfold at sunset. Instead, he had been advised to put down at the Safdarjung airstrip in central Delhi, which was used for microlights and gliders belonging to flying clubs. With the ability to land vertically, the Osprey had no problems setting down.

David and the pilot, whose name he hadn't even asked, had to somehow make their way to the US embassy. David wondered if the embassy would provide any real safety, but it was better than taking one's chances on the streets.

'Kid, what's your name?'

'Stan.' The pilot looked pale and his hands were shaking.

'Get your handgun. Have you ever been in combat before?'

The pilot shook his head, and David wondered why he, of all people, had to babysit this novice.

'Look, just stay close and you'll be fine. When I ask you to shoot at someone, do it, and aim for the head. Got it?'

Stan nodded, his eyes widening at the prospect of being close enough to one of the infected attackers to shoot him or her in the head.

David looked at his GPS. The US embassy was about ten kilometres away. In a straight line and without having to worry about being attacked by crazed mobs, he would have made it there in less than an hour and a half. But now, they would have to trek through a hostile landscape in the dark.

They had been walking for no more than ten minutes when they saw a scene of complete panic. Cars were scattered across the road and people were running in terror.

A group of a dozen or more of the infected walked into view. The streetlights were still on, so David could see the attack unfold clearly. They split into pairs and then attacked their chosen prey, one bringing the target down with a tackle to the leg or waist, and the other then coming in for the bite, usually to the shoulders or neck.

David was stunned by what he saw. The black-turbaned wraiths in front of him were not just mindless zombies; they were actually using at that moment tactics that were well thought-out even if the intelligence was as yet no more than what a pack of wild animals would have demonstrated.

What he saw next was worse. The victims seemed to lie lifeless for a few minutes, and then they got up, transformed into the same kind of creatures who had attacked them.

'Sir, let's get out of here!'

They had probably stayed too long already. It was lucky they hadn't been noticed by the attackers. They began to walk away when a young man ran up to him.

'Sir, please help us!'

The man looked like he had been trying to get home from office. He was wearing a tie and carrying a laptop bag.

This was not David's fight. He just wanted to get to the

embassy and then somehow get back to the United States, so he began to turn away.

'Wait! You're soldiers, you're armed. Please, do something!'

David would have kept going had he not been nearly deafened by the sound of a gun going off inches from his head.

'Shit! Stan, what in god's name are you doing?'

An attacker, who had been approaching the young man from behind, had been hit in the head and keeled over. Stan was standing with his gun in hand, and as another attacker approached, he fired twice, one of the bullets striking the young woman in the head. By now he had attracted the attention of the other creatures, and all of them began approaching them, clambering over the cars that stood between them.

Now, whether he liked it or not, David was in the fight. He selected single-fire on his M4 and brought it up to his eyes. Three carefully aimed pulls on the trigger, three head shots. Their attackers had now stopped, standing in a state of apparent confusion, seemingly surprised at this sudden resistance. That gave the other people there enough time to run.

David looked at Stan and saw a transformed man. Gone was the nervous rookie. Stan was standing straight, holding his gun with both hands, screaming at their attackers to come on. He had often seen battle and stress bring out both the best and the worst in people. It seemed inside Stan there was a brave soldier after all. The problem was that his bravery was likely to get them both killed.

Stan gasped when the ones he had shot in the head got

up after a few minutes, looking even more terrifying with the bleeding bullet holes in their heads. Something that had once been a young woman, dressed in jeans and a bright red T-shirt, leaped over a car and ran straight at Stan, screaming. Stan was too shocked to react, but David put two rounds in her body, which slowed her down, and then a round to her turbaned head.

Stan was now shaking, his bravado slipping away with the realisation of just what they were up against.

'Sir, what do we do now?'

David saw dozens more of the infected now converging on them.

'Now would be a good time to run for our lives.'

They sprinted through the streets, hearing the footsteps of their pursuers just behind them. Every once in a while David would turn and fire a shot or two. Running at full speed, he had no hope of hitting them, least of all in the head, but he hoped that it would at least slow them down. When he saw that it was having no effect, he concentrated on running.

The streetlights were now off, and they had no idea of what lay just a few feet away, let alone whether they were on track to get to the US embassy. For now, immediate survival was about as far as they could plan.

Stan tripped on something and went down with a howl of pain. David's momentum carried him forward a few feet before he turned on his heels to go back to his fallen comrade. He saw that he was too late. Three of the creatures were now almost upon Stan, less than five feet away. David brought his rifle to bear, and with the night scope on, hit two of them on the forehead. Both went down, and the third—a voluptuous woman who must have looked quite striking before her transformation, but was now a bleeding, yellowing monster like the others—took a three-round burst to the chest which sent her reeling back.

'Stan, come on!'

But Stan did not move; instead, he gripped his ankle and looked at David with eyes that were blank with fear. David now saw several more shadows converging on Stan. The young pilot now looked David straight in the eye.

'Sir, please do it. Don't let me become one of them!'

David knew what he was being asked to do, but his hands felt as if they weighed a ton.

Stan screamed again as the first of the wraiths was about to reach him, yellowed and bloodied hands reaching out for him.

'Please, for god's sake. Please.'

David took a deep breath, brought his rifle up and fired a single shot into Stan's head.

A collective howl seemed to emerge from all the creatures around as they realised they had been deprived. The one who had been reaching for Stan crouched over his body and turned his lifeless head in his hands. Then he turned to look at David.

He must have been a middle-aged office-goer, perhaps with a family of his own, no more than a day ago. Now his bloodied, yellow face was contorted with hate, and his clothes were in tatters. The black turban hung precariously from his head as he raised a finger towards David and screamed.

Kaaaaaaaaa...ffffff...rrr.

David selected full auto on his M4 and a dozen 5.56mm

rounds shredded the creature's head. He did not wait to see if it would get up, since a dozen others launched themselves towards him.

He ran as fast as he could, his eyes stinging from the tears that were now running freely down his face.

As soon as the girl had looked up at her and screamed, Hina had run downstairs, aware that she was now in terrible danger. She dragged a sofa to block the front door, hoping it would at least slow the creatures now converging on her house, panting from the exertion, trying to catch her breath.

The window behind her shattered, showering her with glass shards. A yellowed hand reached in and grabbed at her shoulder. In trying to get away, she fell to the ground, and got a closer look at the face that was now peering in at her through the broken window. She saw the crooked glasses, the yellow shirt, and realised with a stifled sob that this creature had till a few minutes ago been Mr Patel, the man from whom she used to buy her groceries. The friendly smile she had known for a dozen years was now replaced by bared, bloody teeth. His face was cut in a dozen places. He had used his head to smash the window. His face was yellow, and the skin seemed to be peeling away in patches and his hate-filled, crazed eyes seemed more like those of a rabid animal than those of a human being. The turban on his head would have looked absurd had Hina not been so terrified.

She heard several hands beating on the door, and then the sofa slowly but surely began to slide back under the onslaught.

Hina had thought of her mortality often. With Imran gone, and her children more a distant memory than a real family, she did not have too much to live for. On the occasional lonely night, she had wondered if she could bring herself to end it all. A bottle of sleeping pills perhaps. But now, faced with a horde of attackers beating down her door, she realised that she wanted to live. Whether or not she had anything to live for, she did not want to go like this. Most certainly, she did not want to become the kind of monster Mr Patel had become.

The front door was now ajar and she saw a foot slip in. The yellow, bloody leg looked incongruous in a high-heeled Gucci shoe, but Hina did not have any time to contemplate that as she got up, looking frantically around for some way to defend herself.

Mayukh's car was bobbing and weaving around the cluttered street, and in other circumstances, he would almost certainly have been stopped on suspicion of drunk driving. Now, all the cops around were either dead or had joined the marauding bands that were rampaging through the city. He braked hard when he saw a body in front of him, lying in the middle of the road. He and his mother looked at it, wondering what they should do. Even though it looked dead, Mayukh could not bring himself to run over another human being. He began to reverse his car so he could drive around it, when the body sat up.

It was a young man, perhaps not much older than Mayukh himself. Except that he was now one of *them*. He launched himself at Mayukh's car, his fingers smashing into the windshield, creating a spider web of cracks inches from Mayukh's face. He began clawing at the glass, trying to get through.

'Drive!'

Mayukh hardly needed the encouragement from his mother. In blind panic, he floored the gas pedal and their Honda City sped forward, carrying their unwelcome passenger with it. His view blocked by the man hanging onto the windshield, Mayukh had no way of knowing what lay ahead, but he hoped that as he picked up speed, the man would be thrown off his hood.

Hina's door was wide open. The streetlights had gone off some minutes earlier, and in the pitch blackness, she could see silhouettes of several figures crowded around the doorway. She knew that her time was up. She closed her eyes and began praying.

There was an ear-splitting crash.

Hina tentatively opened an eye. A car had come to a halt just outside her door, having ploughed through the creatures trying to get to her. Some of them were lying scattered out on the street, and one seemed to be trapped under the car. The rear door of the car had flung open in the crash, and the driver was revving the engine, trying to get away.

Without thinking too much, other than the fact that she was finished if she stayed in her home, Hina ran as fast as she could toward the car and dived in through the open rear door.

Trying to reverse away from the carnage as fast as he could, Mayukh felt the whole car shake as someone landed on the back seat. He spun around, his gun in hand. It was a thin old lady—he had no idea who she was, but she was not one of *them*. He stepped on the gas and the car sped ahead.

They drove in silence for some minutes, each of them still too shocked by what they had endured in the last hour.

Finally, Hina broke the silence. 'I'm Hina Rahman. I am, well I guess I *was*, a history professor.'

Mayukh nodded at her and told her his name. Mrs Ghosh said nothing.

Mayukh looked at his mother, to see what shape she was in. Her hands were shaking and she was continuously trying to call his father on her mobile, but all the networks seemed to be down. She finally threw the phone hard on the floor and began whimpering.

Hina reached out and held her shoulder. This simple act of compassion seemed to make his mother collapse into loud sobs.

Mayukh's mind was blank. He was more terrified than he had ever been, but somewhere, he still had hope—hope that this was somehow all a bad dream he would wake up from, hope that there surely was some government in control somewhere. The world as he knew it couldn't all just end, could it? He looked at his mother.

'Mom, we just need to get to the stadium. The army will be there. Whatever this infection is, they will contain it and find a cure. All we need to do is get to the stadium and we'll be okay.'

Mrs Ghosh seemed to take some heart at his words. They drove on, their car's headlights the only illumination in the dark streets around them.

David was on a cycle he had found abandoned by the roadside, still trying to get to the US embassy. There was no way of knowing whether it would actually offer any safety, but it was not as if he had any better options.

After ten minutes of riding, he realised that it would be suicidal to continue in the darkness. *They* owned the night; all around him, he could see groups of the infected gather, and while he could outrun them with none of the streetlights on, it was but a matter of time before he stumbled into one of them.

He stopped near what appeared to be a cluster of shops. With his small flashlight, he saw a broken sign which said 'Khan Market'. Not seeing anyone around, David figured his best bet was to hunker down for the night, and then proceed in daytime. That was unless the creatures were now active during the day as well.

He walked around the shops cautiously, using the night scope on his M4 to check for any sign of trouble. The market seemed abandoned.

After a few minutes of walking, he came upon, of all things, a McDonalds. He realised, suddenly, that he was very hungry, and the prospect of eating something other than MREs was, despite everything, exciting. He kicked in the door and went in, sweeping the room in front of him with his rifle. There was nobody there, but it looked like the staff had left in a hurry—food was strewn around in the kitchen.

David barricaded the door with tables and then went upstairs, where he finally took a breather after a day in which he had spent every single minute trying to stay alive. He bit into a burger, and looked out the window. He was done with running for now. He would spend the night here, but there was going to be precious little rest. He couldn't afford to let his guard down.

He ate a couple of burgers, drank some Coke and then unslung his backpack. He set his rifle against a window that offered the best view of the road outside. He knew that he had to conserve the batteries of his night vision scopes, so he turned it off. He would switch it on only if he really needed to.

He saw a group of the infected, perhaps twenty-strong, walk on the main road, some five hundred metres away, before they ran into one of the housing complexes nearby. He heard screams coming from the darkened houses, and he tried to block them out. He spent the next few minutes just staring out the window, hoping that none of the mobs came towards him.

As much as he tried not to succumb to it, fatigue and stress got the better of him, and he fell into an uneasy slumber.

Mayukh had never seen the city so dark before. All the streetlights were off, and none of the houses or shops lining the road had their lights on. Even if some of them had generators, Mayukh guessed the occupants had switched off all their lights so as not to draw attention to themselves. Nobody knew whether light attracted the infected.

That was the dilemma in which he found himself. Without his headlights on, he could barely see what was on the road ahead of him, yet he knew that his headlights would be a magnet for any of the marauding bands of the infected now rampaging through the city. He didn't even know what he should call them. Were they zombies? He shook off the thought, reasoning that giving them a name would only make this nightmare more real.

He glanced at his mother. She had dozed off, the stress proving too much for her. The professor in the backseat had not spoken for many minutes.

After a few minutes, Mayukh saw a faint glow on the horizon. As they got closer, he realised that the light was coming from the giant floodlights installed at the stadium. If the lights at the stadium were still on, it could mean only one thing—that someone was still in control there.

'Mom, look there!'

As his mother opened her eyes and looked at the looming lights, Mayukh threw caution to the wind. He turned on the headlights and accelerated. They were so close to safety; he was confident they could beat any mob trying to pursue them on foot.

Within seconds they were at the stadium. Bunkers dotted the perimeter, with gun barrels sticking out of several of them. A few metres ahead of them were men in army uniforms standing in the shadows. The sign in the middle of the road said, 'Proceed on foot from here.'

They could drive no further anyway, since the road was blocked with barbed wire, so they got out of the car, looking anxiously around them for attackers. Not seeing anyone, they broke into a run towards the soldiers.

Hina was the first to notice something was wrong. In a situation like this, surely the soldiers would be carrying guns? She was about to shout out a warning, when shadows leapt out of the bunkers to their right.

Mayukh was just feet away from the nearest soldier when he came to a screeching halt. The man who turned to face him was wearing an army uniform all right, but his skin was the now all-too-familiar yellow as he shook a bloodied finger at Mayukh.

Mrs Ghosh was just behind him and as the man leapt at him, she pushed Mayukh out of the way, going down with the man on top of her. Mayukh rolled on the ground and as he tried to get up, more of the creatures were now converging on the prone figure of his mother. How could he help her? The gun was still in the car. He jumped up and rushed towards her.

Mrs Ghosh looked at him and shouted, 'Please run! Run! Hina, take him!'

A couple of the creatures turned towards him, baring their teeth. Before they could attack, Mrs Ghosh grabbed hold of their legs, terror giving her desperate strength.

Hina's arms stopped Mayukh in his headlong rush towards his mother. 'No, let go of me! Let me go!'

Hina slapped him hard, and he looked at her, shocked.

'Mayukh, she gave her life so you could live. Don't let her sacrifice be for nothing. Let's go!'

She half pulled, half dragged Mayukh to the car. She pushed him into the passenger seat, got into the driver's seat, backed the car out of the approach road, and drove away as fast as she could.

Mayukh sat next to her, his head between his legs, sobbing in absolute agony.

FOUR

Rose was dressed in one of those flowery dresses that she liked so much.

'Baby, you must be so tired. Let me make it better.'

She was kneeling over him, holding his hands in her own. He reached out to caress her hair, and then he saw that her hair had come out in clumps in his hand. He looked up to see her face. It wasn't his Rose anymore. Her skin had yellowed; the impish smile had been replaced by a feral grin, white sockets where her blue eyes were.

'Baby, come to me,' the creature who had been Rose crooned again.

David woke up, covered in sweat and shaking. He took a minute to calm down and remind himself where he was. As much as he tried to reassure himself that Rose was okay, his mind kept replaying the nightmare he had just seen.

He heard the sound of a car approaching. He looked at his watch—it was now almost one in the morning and only someone very stupid or very desperate would be out at this time. For a split second he considered whether *they* might have learned to drive, and then dismissed the thought. He put his eye to the scope of his assault rifle and turned the night vision optics on.

About a kilometre away, plainly visible in the greenish glow of the night-vision, was a car driving slowly down the road. It had its headlights off, which perhaps explained the driver's caution.

David involuntarily shrunk back as he saw four figures leap out from the side of the road and jump on to the car. The car swerved from left to right, either in an attempt to shake off the attackers, or because the driver had given into absolute panic.

Out of instinct, more than anything else, David tracked in on one of the attackers with his M4 rifle. With the car moving erratically, it was far from an easy shot, and he certainly could not guarantee a shot to the head, but he knew he would not miss.

Then he stopped himself. What was he thinking? This was not his fight. All he needed to do was wait the night out in his hiding place and get to the embassy in the morning.

The car braked hard. The attacker clinging onto the hood was thrown hard to the ground. The car accelerated, running over his prone body and continuing down the road. Another form clinging to the left door, the billowing embroidered sari looking incongruous on the mindless killer's body, was thrown off. That left two attackers, one on each side of the car.

David watched through his scope as the car came closer, now no more than fifty metres away. The driver had done well so far, and something in him thought it would be a terrible waste of a brave person if the attackers got to whoever was inside. He caught a glimpse of the driver now. It was a woman, and she had a young man next to her. Perhaps a mother and son.

To serve and protect.

He had sworn to defend the innocent, and all his training overcame any thought of self-preservation. Whether it was his fight or not, he could not sit back and watch a family be slaughtered. He already knew that the infected brutally killed those who resisted.

One of the infected tried to claw his way into the car through the smashed passenger-side window. Before he had even consciously decided to help, David's finger pressed lightly on the trigger.

Hina was screaming at the top of her lungs. All the bravery or desperation that had kept her going till now had dissipated. Seeing the two yellow, decayed faces with their deformed teeth and features glaring at her from each side of the car, she felt that her time was over. Mayukh was still in shock, and had made no attempt to use the gun that was lying by his side. Hina hadn't even bothered to reach for it. She had never held a gun in her hands, and didn't think she would increase their chances of survival by trying to use one for the first time when under attack by these fiends.

She realised she was running out of road and turned to face the attacker on her right. He had lost his turban in the chase, and his head was half bald, patches of yellow scalp showing. He looked no more than fifteen. A boy who had perhaps been playing games with his friends a day earlier. What a waste of a life. What a waste of all the lives.

Before she could think any further, the boy fell off the car as if an invisible flyswatter had swatted him away. She looked behind to see him sitting up, and then another hammer blow knocked him flat. When she turned to her left, the same fate had befallen the attacker there. She was so transfixed by the sight that she noticed too late that she was heading straight into some parked cars.

Hina was thrown forward by the impact, hitting her head on the dashboard. She reeled back in pain, and her hand came away wet with her blood when she put it to her forehead. She looked behind her to see if the attackers had followed them, but in the darkness, she could only see their prone bodies lying on the road some fifty metres behind.

Then the door opened and before she could scream, strong hands wrapped around her mouth and pulled her out.

Mayukh was huddled in a corner of the room, only just recovering from the blackout he'd sunk into after his head hit the windshield. As he came to, he heard some voices whispering a few feet away from him. He tried to make out what they were saying.

'Captain, what's your plan?'

'Ma'am, just call me David. I'm on my way to the US embassy tomorrow at first light when these creatures aren't about. You could come with me till there. I wish I could do more for you, but I do need to get out and back to my family.'

'You've done more than enough for us, young man. And you can call me Hina.'

Mayukh tried to clear the cobwebs of his mind. Was he having a bad dream? Would his mother come and wake him up now, reminding him that once again he was going to be late for school?

His mother.

He sat up with a jolt as everything that had happened in the day came back to him. As it all sank in, he slumped back against the wall and looked blankly at the floor.

He sensed someone sitting down next to him. He was holding something that he pressed into Mayukh's hand.

'Young man, that's a fine gun you have there. I picked it up from the car. Would have been a shame to leave it there.'

Mayukh looked down to see his father's pistol. Strong hands gripped his arm.

'Look, I've lost a lot of good men recently. Men who were like brothers to me, but none of that compares to your loss.'

The man got up and walked to the open window, through which Mayukh could see the faint light of daybreak.

Hina was by his side. She had a bandage on her forehead, and was trying hard to smile, though Mayukh could see her eyes creased with fatigue and stress.

'Here, have some breakfast.'

She held out some cold French fries and a burger which Mayukh wolfed down. He was so famished, it tasted like the best meal he had ever had. She ran her hand through his hair, and as Mayukh looked at her he was reminded of his grandmother. The same kind eyes, the same smile.

'That man there is an American soldier. He saved us last night and he'll help us get to the American embassy. We can try to contact someone in the government and find out where we can go that is safe.'

Mayukh nodded mutely.

When David announced that they were leaving, Mayukh followed him, his body going through the motions, but his mind totally numb and blank.

David examined the car that he had rescued Hina and Mayukh from. It had been a close call. They had made it back into the restaurant moments before the attackers he had shot had regained consciousness. He opened the boot and whistled at all the canned food stuffed into it.

'Kid, your folks sure were well prepared. No telling what we'll run into, so help me carry this stuff into another car. I guess today people will forgive us for borrowing their car.'

David chose an SUV and had started to load the things into the back when Hina turned to him. 'David, wouldn't we be able to move through the streets easier in a smaller car. There are cars and ... things ...'

She couldn't bring herself to say *bodies,* but it was clear that was what she meant.

David shrugged. 'Maybe, but if I have run through or over things, this will come in handy.'

Mayukh stood quietly on one side.

David whispered to Hina, 'I hope the kid gets his senses back. He's in shock, and I understand that, but he will get himself killed real fast if he doesn't snap out of it soon.'

'The poor boy has been through hell.'

David finished loading the last of the cans and got into the car. 'Hina, I think we haven't begun to see what hell looks like yet.'

The city, as they drove through it, was the opposite of what Hina had expected—and it frightened her even more if that was possible. After the events of the previous night, she had feared there would be carnage and death all around. Instead, the city was deserted, and that made it even more unsettling. There was no sign of a single living soul around, nor any signs of bodies. There were just cars and bikes scattered all around where their drivers had left them, and dark patches that indicated where people had been brought down. She had never heard the city this quiet. No car horns honking, no rumble of traffic, no people chattering away on their mobile phones. She longed for all the things that she may have once complained about.

She glanced at Mayukh, who was sitting in the backseat. He was still quiet, but at least he appeared to be coming out of his shock. The young heal fast, she reasoned, and then took her first close look at their driver. In the darkness of night, she had barely had a chance to see who their saviour was.

Her first reaction was that he looked so young. He had close-cropped blonde hair, and a face that made him look no older than a kid just graduating from college. She knew better, after having seen what he had done the previous night, and the only real hint to the fact that he was a trained killer lay in his eyes. They seemed ever alert, constantly scanning their surroundings for any sign of trouble. Hina knew that he would probably be on his way to the US soon enough, but was glad to have his company while it lasted. A boy in shock and an old professor—she and Mayukh didn't have much chance of surviving on their own.

David spotted some movement to their right and his hands tightened on the steering wheel as they entered what would have normally been the crowded roundabouts of

Barakhamba Road. He didn't know if the infected could be out in daylight, but he was not about to find out the hard way.

The road ahead was blocked by cars, and resembled a surreal maze that he was trying to pick his way through, so there was no question of driving any faster than a slow trot. He forced aside a bike using the bulk of the SUV he was driving, but realised he would have no option but to weave around the cars in front of him.

Again he spotted some movement on his right. It seemed to be a small shopping complex, with broken signs that announced a salon, an internet café and a pharmacy, among other signs in Hindi. As a special forces operator, he was almost fluent in Urdu and had a working knowledge of Hindi, but trying to read the Hindi words would have required more attention than he could spare.

He was now sure of it—there were at least two people moving inside what remained of the internet café on the ground floor. The door was closed, but the windows were shattered and he could see shadows moving in the darkness inside.

He turned to Mayukh. 'Kid, see that internet café there, fifty metres to the right?'

He didn't get a response.

'I think I saw someone moving inside it. No idea who it could be, but just take out your gun and cover that area. I don't want to stop or take my attention off the road.'

Assuming Mayukh was doing as he had asked, David focussed his attention on the road ahead. A split second later, he saw a head peek out from behind the shattered windows of the café and caught a glint of something that may well have been a weapon. He turned to see Mayukh slumped in the rear seat, the gun lying uselessly by his side.

'Damn it!'

David stopped the SUV and brought up his M4, scanning the area to his right for any imminent threat. With the crowded road ahead, if they were up against attackers with weapons, he would never be able to get away in time. He had far better chances sticking around and counting on his training and firepower.

A tuft of silvery hair showed at the window and a face emerged. David could hear Hina gasp behind him. He had his sight trained on the head. At any sign of trouble, he would put a round through the forehead.

As the man emerged, David put his finger on the trigger and then brought his gun down, exhaling loudly in relief. 'What's going on? Who are they?'

David had his head back against the seat, thankful that he had not fired. Hina looked over his shoulder and saw who had been hiding in the shop.

They were an ancient couple, perhaps no younger than eighty, dressed in rags. It was likely they had lived in one of the nearby slums, and when the chaos began, had sought refuge in the shops. Both the man and woman looked around uncomprehendingly, with blank, terrified eyes. Hina guessed that they perhaps had no idea of how it had happened—how, one day, ordinary people had turned into bloodthirsty monsters.

The couple stumbled towards them, holding out their hands as if seeking help. Hina started to speak, but David cut her off, guessing what she was about to say.

'No, we can't take them with us.'

'But, look at them ...'

In response, David got out of the vehicle and, opening the back, took out some of the canned and packaged food, which he handed over to the old man. The man smiled his thanks, his eyes welling up.

'That was a nice thing you did,' Hina said as they drove away.

David just grunted and kept his focus on the road. Without looking back, he addressed Mayukh.

'Kid, you need to decide whether you want to stay alive or not. If they had been attackers, we could have been in big trouble. In a few minutes, I'll be on my way, and won't see you again. But here's some friendly advice—snap out of it, otherwise you'll get yourself and Hina in big trouble.'

As they drove into the heart of Delhi, past India Gate and then onwards towards the diplomatic enclaves, they began to see signs of other survivors. A family walking on the roadside, a group of young men carrying rods and swords, two policemen walking around as if wondering what they should do. The entire city seemed to be in shock, but there was no sign of the infected attackers who had wreaked so much havoc the previous night. It was as if they had disappeared at first light.

They drove by the prime minister's residence, and saw that it was totally deserted. There was not a single policeman in sight. Hina wondered whether that was because the prime minister had been evacuated or because even he had not escaped the chaos.

'We're here, folks.'

Hina looked up at David's words to see the high walls of the US embassy. The gate was shut, but there was no sign of anyone around. David drove right up to the gate, and pandemonium erupted all around them.

'Freeze! Stop the vehicle and keep your hands where I can see them!'

David did as he was told, and Hina followed suit. A second later, a fully-armed US marine appeared, assault rifle at the ready. He seemed awfully young, and his rifle shook unsteadily in his hands. He looked at David and took in his uniform and stripes.

'You in the US army?'

David snorted dismissively, looking at the soldier's name tag.

'Private Shafer, I'm a SEAL. And that's *sir* to you.'

The man stood straight and saluted, as if relieved to have someone who could take charge. He pointed at Hina and Mayukh.

'What about them?'

'They're with me, for now.'

The marine opened the gates and David drove in. As soon as he got out, the marine ran up, eager to learn what had happened outside. David asked incredulously, 'Where are the others? Don't tell me you're the only one around.'

The marine answered, his voice now betraying his fear, 'Sir, all the senior diplomats and families left day before. They left me here to guard the last diplomat. They told me we'd be evacuated yesterday, and then everything went to hell. We just turned off all the lights and hid in the basement.'

'That's the best anyone could have done. So don't be too hard on yourself, soldier. Now, where's the diplomat?'

David was led inside where he saw a man crouched behind a desk, burning documents in a fireplace.

'Excuse me, sir. I'm Captain David Bremsak, US Navy SEALs. I was told you're the ranking diplomat here. Could you tell me what our plans for evacuation are?'

The man turned to face him, and David drew back in shock. He was red-faced and visibly drunk as he struggled to get up. As he came closer, David could smell the alcohol on his breath.

'Captain, I'm Jeremy Abbot. I'm the frigging cultural attaché here, which means I'm the CIA spook.'

The man laughed and David wondered just how unhinged the man had been by the pressure to talk so loosely.

'Captain, if you're here to get help, I'm afraid this is the only help I can provide.' He motioned to a half-empty bottle of Black Label on the table behind him.

Abbot continued, 'Just got a transmission. No help coming our way. They asked me to stay behind and ensure all our dirty work is destroyed. It seems those bloody secrets about whom we're spying on are more valuable than expendable old me. And now they realise they can't get any of us out ... they're saying all existing air assets anywhere near here are either incapacitated by the outbreak or being withdrawn to prevent further spread of the infection.'

David was shattered by the news, but something in what the man said gave him a surge of hope.

'Your radio's working? Someone's still transmitting?'

Abbot shrugged and took a swig straight from the bottle.

'Don't get your hopes up. Just a burst this morning, telling all overseas personnel to stay where they are, and that people are working on plans. Basically, we've been left to rot.'

David had asked the marine if he wanted to come along with them, but the young soldier had said he'd stay at his post. David thought he was being stupid, but had to admire his courage.

They drove around for a few minutes, all of them silent, trying to reconcile to the fact that there did not seem to be any help headed their way. If there was a government in control anywhere, it had given up on this corner of the world.

Finally, Hina broke the silence. 'David, it's past noon now. We need to have a plan for how to survive the night.'

David stopped the car. When Hina looked at him, she was truly frightened for the first time since she had met him. So far, he had exuded nothing but quiet confidence, and with his obvious training and firepower, she had come to regard him as something of a safety blanket.

But now his eyes were downcast, his shoulders slumped. He slammed his fist hard against the steering wheel in frustration.

Hina looked on, ever more afraid as she saw the first cracks appear in David's confidence. Then, as if with a conscious effort of will, David took a deep breath, and his settled, calm look was back.

'Let's take it one step at a time. First, we need a place to stay where we can be safe.'

They were now driving towards Connaught Place, and Hina saw the Imperial Hotel to her left.

'How about a hotel?'

David shook his head, with a slight smile.

'I'm sure we could get a room or two. I doubt they're fully booked. But it's not a good place to hide in. Too many entry points, and if we're cornered, we've got no place to run.'

They drove around at a slow crawl, manoeuvring around the cars abandoned haphazardly on the road. Hina spotted Oxford Bookstore, a part of her mind wondering how her new novel was faring. Writing had been such an integral part of her life, yet after just one day, it seemed like it had been a totally different life altogether.

David saw what she was looking at and misinterpreted what was going through her mind.

'Hina, you should have been in the army! That's a perfect place—slightly off the main road, just one main entrance and that too through a staircase, and I'm sure they have a rear exit in case we need it.'

Hina didn't bother correcting him, happy that they seemed to have identified a refuge, and also because being near books would in some way bring back her life the way it had been.

David decided that leaving all their supplies in the vehicle was too risky, so they carried the cans and bags inside. Mayukh did his part in silence, and when they were inside, he retreated to a corner and sat down.

Hina stood in front of the bestseller rack, looking at her novel, currently in fifth place. She took a copy and felt the soft edges, smelled the paper, and it was almost easy to believe that the world had not been transformed into a place roamed by bloodthirsty maniacs infected by some unknown disease; that people still had the time and luxury to spend hours reading stories like the one she had written—of a British traveller finding adventure and love in Mughal India.

David walked up behind her, and looked at the novel she had in her hand, with its cover of a rugged-looking man and a voluptuous woman in a torn sari. 'I'm not much of a reader, but I could never figure out how anyone could read trashy romances like that. Some dirty old man must be sitting somewhere, churning out stories like that.'

Hina almost choked at his words. She looked at him, a broad smile on her face.

'Captain, the trashy novel I hold in my hand was written by a very dirty old woman. Me.'

David looked at Hina, sure that she was pulling his leg. When she didn't flinch, he exclaimed, 'No friggin' way!'

When she told him her secret, he doubled over laughing, and she joined in, the two of them laughing so hard their stomachs hurt.

Afterwards, David barricaded the rear exit and satisfied himself that the front entrance could be secured. Between the front entrance, and the store's main door was a small space. The main door could not be the primary point of defence since it was set some feet away from the head of the stairs, so he decided to leave the door open, which would hopefully serve to make anyone assume that nobody was inside. He set up a firing position just outside and to the left of the main door—a podium stacked with books, with enough space in between for him to fire through. He also placed his single Claymore anti-personnel mine just outside the main door, facing outwards, but did not activate it. That would be their last-ditch effort at defence.

When he came back in, he found Hina curled up with a book in her hand. So far, he had been very impressed with how well she had coped with the situation, given her age and what she had been through. Then he spotted Mayukh sitting glumly in a corner. He remembered the scene back in the SUV when Mayukh had failed to cover them, and trying hard to control his anger, he walked over to the boy and sat down next to him.

'How're you doing?'

There was no response.

David took a deep breath, trying to control himself. He didn't have kids himself, and in the company of hard men in the SEALs, the way to deal with a young rookie who was losing it involved several push-ups, runs with a heavy pack, and throwing them out if they could not make it. None of those were options right now, so he tried to see if he could get through to the boy next to him.

'Look, kid, I know you've been through a lot, but now we need to pull ourselves together if we have to survive.'

Mayukh looked towards him and simply said, 'I'm not a kid. Stop calling me that. My name is Mayukh.'

David wanted to reach out and slap him, but he controlled himself.

'Okay, Mayukh. You do realise we aren't in a normal situation, don't you? What you did in the car could have gotten us all killed. Do you realise that? We've all been through crap—but now, we have to stick together and you need to help out.'

Mayukh buried his head in his hands for a few moments, and when he finally raised it, David saw that his eyes were beginning to well up with tears.

'David, do you know the last thing my father told me? He said he hoped I could be the man he had always dreamt I would be.'

David watched in silence.

Mayukh continued, finally opening up, finally coming to grips with what he had gone through.

'Forget being a man, I couldn't even protect my mother. She's gone because of me. I've always been useless. What the hell am I good for, anyway? You're the big bad soldier who knows what to do. I'm just a screwed-up kid. Maybe I should just take my gun and kill myself.'

It finally dawned on David just what demons the boy was dealing with, and he held him gently by the shoulder.

'Mayukh, I don't have a son, so I can't begin to understand everything you're going through. But my dad died when I was about your age, and I've been holding a gun and going into harm's way since I was not much older than you. I've led young men like you into battle, and I've been young and scared enough to wet my pants when I first saw combat.'

Mayukh was now listening.

'Look, I'm no braver than you are. But what I've learnt is that "being a man", as your father said, boils down to one simple thing—watching out for the guy next to you. That's what kept me and my boys going even when the shit hit the fan. And now, whether we like it or not, this is our unit. We need to look out for each other, even if we hardly know or even like each other—we have nothing and nobody else. I can fight, but I don't know the city, so I need you as much as you need me. Think about that.'

David walked over to another corner, leaving Mayukh alone to consider what he had just said.

It was five in the evening. Hina and David conferred and decided that they would not risk any light at night; they would have an early dinner.

Dinner was a can of baked beans and some potato chips, washed down with apple juice, and when they finished, David turned to Hina.

'You guys rest inside. I'll be outside watching the road.'

He had knelt behind the podium, with his rifle ready, when he felt a tap on his shoulder.

It was Mayukh.

'David, why don't you rest for a change? I'll watch for a while.'

David looked over Mayukh's shoulder to see a slight grin on Hina's face.

'Sure. Look, right now we can still see with the naked eye. Once it gets dark enough that we need to use the night vision scope, I'll replace you. Cool?'

Mayukh nodded, and with his handgun beside him, took up position.

David passed Hina as he went inside the bookstore.

'The kid's tougher than I thought.'

Hina smiled in reply. 'David, none of us is tough till we are tested. I think he'll be okay. Get some rest now.'

As David went inside, she heard him chuckling.

'What's so funny?'

David turned, trying not to laugh.

'I can't get over the fact that *you* write that stuff. Man, I flicked through a few pages. *His eager hands fumbled with the knot of her sari.* Yikes, you are a dirty old woman!'

Hina laughed as the soldier curled up in a corner and in less than five minutes was sound asleep. She read for a while, and then when the light got too dim, she also decided to rest. She had no idea what the hours or days ahead held for her, but for the first time in two days, she felt relatively secure.

David dreamt of Rose, and of talking to his own son, telling him to be a man. He knew Rose wanted kids, and he had always been noncommittal, and in his dream, he remembered swearing that if he got back to her, they would have an army of kids.

That was when he was awakened by the sounds of screaming outside.

FIVE

David picked up his M4, switched off the safety and went outside in a crouch.

Hina was near the doorway, looking out in the fading light. He asked her to get down, and then he reached Mayukh, who was sitting behind the podium.

'What's going on?'

He heard the scream again, and when he looked for its source, he saw three figures struggling on the road some twenty metres away, just outside the perimeter fence of the complex where the bookstore was. David looked up and saw that the sun had still not fully set.

'It can't be *them*. At least, it shouldn't be yet.'

He looked through his scope to see what was going on, and it became obvious what was happening. Two men were trying to grab a young girl, who was doing her best to fight them off. Mayukh asked to see as well.

When David put the rifle down, Mayukh looked at him, as if seeking direction.

David was torn. 'Mayukh, people are probably going crazy all over the world. They are looting, raping and murdering at will while daylight lasts, since they figure there's no more law to punish them, and not much of a future to look forward to. We can't stop them all.'

The girl was putting up a hell of a fight, but it would be just a matter of time before she was overpowered.

Before David could think anything else, he saw a blur out of the corner of his eyes. It was Mayukh running towards the road.

'Mayukh, stop!'

David raised his rifle, but with Mayukh directly between him and the men, he did not have a clean shot. With the Barrett, he could have risked taking out the men without harming the girl, but all he had with him was his M4, and he could not guarantee a clean shot at such range, with the girl and the men so close together. He groaned and then ran after Mayukh.

The two men had been so intent on overpowering the girl that they did not see Mayukh run at them. Before they had a chance to react, Mayukh had raised the handgun and fired one shot in the air. Everyone seemed to freeze for a minute as the unnatural quiet of the city further amplified the gunshot.

'Get away from her!'

Mayukh had his gun pointed at the men. He had never shot a person before, and certainly didn't want to do so now. He hoped that the threat would be enough to deter the two men.

As he walked closer, he observed several details. The girl was no older than him, and was dressed in a school uniform, which was now torn at the right shoulder. Blood covered most of the right side of her face. Hiding behind her was a boy no more than two or three years old, clutching a toy car.

The two men were now facing him, and both were swaying unsteadily. As one of them spat in his direction, Mayukh realised that both were blind drunk. One of them slurred in Hindi as he walked toward Mayukh.

'The demons will be out again in a few minutes. Let's have some fun with her while we can. Join us if you want.'

Mayukh's hands were shaking, but he tried to keep his voice steady.

'Look, I don't want to hurt you. Just leave her alone and go.'

The larger of the two men took a step towards him, flipping out a switchblade.

'Look boy, I have killed many men, some in prison. Get lost before I kill you and then rape her.'

David was crouched behind the perimeter wall, and while he couldn't quite hear what was being said, the actions of the men were clear enough. He had his rifle raised to his shoulder, his finger on the trigger. All it would take was a little bit of pressure and the man closest to Mayukh would die.

The man advanced on Mayukh, raising his knife as if to bring it down. David tensed, ready to fire, when he heard a gunshot.

The man collapsed to the ground, holding his leg and screaming in pain. David saw the smoking gun in Mayukh's hand as he walked over to the man and kicked the knife away.

'I don't want to kill you, but if I shoot you in the other leg as well, you won't even be able to run or hide when *they* come out.'

The man kept howling, holding his bleeding left leg.

Mayukh turned to the second man, who had now dropped all his bravado and had his hands up.

'Take your friend and get out of here.'

Mayukh kept his gun raised as the man picked up his companion and struggled across the road. When they were on the other side, he motioned to the girl to follow him. When she hesitated, he just pointed to the sun.

'We don't have time for formal introductions. Come on.'

He walked back towards the bookstore, followed by the girl and the toddler holding her hand. When Mayukh passed David, he saw the soldier had a bemused smile on his face.

'I never figured you'd go Rambo on us,' he said, observing the transformation in the boy. The weak, traumatised child was gone. Mayukh's eyes were steady and confident, almost challenging David to mock him.

'You said we need to watch out for each other. That's what I intend to do.'

David followed him back inside, gripped with a feeling he had experienced many times before—the mixed emotions when he saw another sensitive, caring young man turn into someone who could take a life.

By the time they entered the bookstore, the sun had almost set. David took position outside, watching for trouble through the greenish hues of his night vision optics. Hina tended to the girl's wounds, and was relieved to find they were only superficial cuts.

Mayukh was sitting in a corner, still shaking a bit from the adrenaline rush of what had just happened, when the little boy walked up to him. Mayukh got his first good look at him. Curly hair framed his chubby face and his eager, bright eyes. He was wearing a crumpled Mickey Mouse t-shirt and khaki shorts.

'Are you Batman?'

Mayukh didn't know how to respond to the question so he just shook his head. The boy smiled, showing prominent dimples.

'Good. I don't like Batman. I think you're Pete.'

Mayukh had no idea what the boy was talking about but smiled back. He was taken aback when the boy sat down next to him and leaned against him, placing his head on Mayukh's shoulder. Mayukh had never been around small children, and he had no idea of what to do or say. He asked the boy if he wanted something to eat.

The boy's eyes lit up. 'Ice cream.'

Mayukh reluctantly told him there was no ice cream to be had, and was horrified when the little boy's lip quivered, and he seemed to be on the verge of tears.

He was grateful when the girl came up and sat down next to them, speaking to the boy in a soft voice. 'Abhi, we don't have ice cream now. We'll have some tomorrow. Okay?'

The boy seemed to be fine with that; he took out his small red toy car from his pocket and got busy playing with it.

The girl turned to face Mayukh. 'Thanks for helping us.'

Mayukh nodded.

'Abhi is my kid brother. He'll turn three in a month, and when he calls anyone Pete, it's the ultimate compliment.'

Mayukh shrugged. He still had no idea what she was talking about.

She smiled. 'I guess you don't have a kid brother or sister. Mickey Mouse Clubhouse, the big guy Pete? Abhi loves him because he's the biggest and strongest of them all. As for my promise of ice cream, anything in the future for him is tomorrow and anything that has happened in the past happened yesterday.'

Abhi smiled a cherubic smile at Mayukh, as if sharing a big secret. 'I will have ice cream tomorrow.'

Mayukh held his hand out towards the girl. 'I'm sorry. I haven't even introduced myself. My name is Mayukh.'

'Hi, I'm Swati.'

Her smile was replaced by a sudden look of vulnerability and it was a moment before she regained her composure.

'Who would have thought ...' The rest of her sentence was swallowed in a stifled sob.

Mayukh tentatively held her shoulder as she continued. 'Our parents were taken the first night. We hid in the closet and since then I've been trying to keep Abhi safe. Thanks for saving me.'

Mayukh took a closer look at her face in the fading light that was still coming in from the open front door. Her black hair was tied back in a ponytail, and if they had been in the same school, Mayukh could imagine she would have been the object of every boy's affection, with her sharp, pretty features. But her eyes were glowing, even defiant, and for a moment, Mayukh felt ashamed of the weakness he had shown over the last day. Unarmed and alone, this girl had maintained her courage and composure, while he had broken down. He shrank back against the wall, suddenly very ashamed of himself.

Swati saw his expression and somehow seemed to read his mind. 'Mayukh, I don't know what happened before we met, but we wouldn't be alive if you hadn't helped us. So if Abhi thinks you're Pete, he's right. You're his hero.'

As she got up to walk towards Hina, she added softly, 'And mine.'

Swati and Abhi had their dinner of cookies and canned fruit in near total darkness. Abhi wouldn't leave Mayukh's side, even insisting that he feed him. He kept up an incessant chatter about Disney characters, cars he liked, how much he loved chocolate chip cookies ... Mayukh was clueless about most of what Abhi was going on about, but it didn't seem to matter.

'See McQueen, he goes so fast!' Abhi exclaimed as he raced his toy car over Mayukh's leg.

Hina looked at Mayukh and smiled. 'You seem to have got your own little fan there.'

Mayukh could only grin back. He had never been around kids much, but now, looking at the curly-haired bundle of energy next to him, he felt fiercely protective. He reached over, tousling Abhi's hair.

'Don't you need to sleep now?'

Abhi looked up at him with big, innocent eyes. 'But I need a new diaper and milk.'

Totally out of his depth now, Mayukh looked towards Swati for help. She came over, grinning from ear to ear.

'He normally doesn't take to strangers this easily. You must have made quite an impression. Come on, Abhi, no new diaper today. Let's go to sleep now.'

Abhi burst into tears, bawling at the top of his voice. Swati tried to hush him and looked at Mayukh and Hina apologetically.

'I'm sorry, but he's used to sleeping in a fresh diaper. He's not potty-trained yet, and he always has milk at bedtime.'

Hina immediately went to the bathroom to see if she could rustle up something, and then came back with some toilet paper.

'This is all we have. And no milk of course.'

Swati tried comforting Abhi, but the boy kept crying. She looked at Mayukh, an almost apologetic expression in her eyes.

David came inside, and whispered to Mayukh, 'We need to calm him down. *They* hear that crying, and we're in big trouble.'

Mayukh realised that somehow he had been given charge of Abhi, and also that he did not really mind it. He looked out the door and saw something across the street.

'David, just cover my back.'

'Where are you going? It's past sunset.'

Mayukh answered over his shoulder to Hina, 'I see a pharmacy, and it's just a few feet away. I'll see if they have anything there.'

He wondered if David would stop him, but the soldier just tapped him on his back and said, 'Be quick, and stay sharp. If there's any sign of trouble, aim for the head.'

Mayukh slipped into the darkness, gun in hand and a flashlight tucked into his belt. He realised that, after just one day, his eyes were able to adjust quickly to the darkness.

The sky was clear, perhaps the one positive effect of all the cars and factories being silent, and in the moonlight, he could see quite well. Now that he was outside, he felt a stab of panic. David was a trained soldier who knew what he was doing, but Mayukh was just a kid in school who may have liked to play soldier on video games, but had no clue what to do in dangerous situations in real life.

He gripped the gun with both hands, partly to steady them but also to give himself confidence. He crept across the road, looking around for any sign of movement. With his heart hammering, he entered the store and turned on his flashlight to see what was inside. Much of the store had been looted, but to his delight, he found what he wanted—several packs of Pampers. He'd had no idea diaper packs could be so bulky, and he realised that carrying even just two meant he would not be able to hold his gun in his hand. He looked around frantically for bags and finally found a large black garbage bag. He put two large packs of diapers in it as well as several packets of what looked to be baby milk powder. Then he went back out into the darkness.

He was halfway to the bookstore when he thought he heard voices in the distance. All his bravado gone, he ran at a full sprint, entering the open door panting for breath.

As he handed the bag to Hina, she looked in and chuckled. 'I think he's a bit big for an M size.'

Mayukh rolled his eyes.

'I'm kidding, Mayukh. That was a very brave thing to do.'

Hina started making some milk for Abhi while Swati sat down next to Mayukh. In the darkness, he could barely see her face, but she held his hand and squeezed it lightly.

'Thanks again.'

Before he could say anything, Abhi ran up and hugged his knee.

'I want him to put me to sleep.'

And so, Mayukh sat down with Abhi as he drank his milk and then the little boy put his head on Mayukh's lap.

'Can you tell me a story?'

Mayukh looked around for help, but could only hear Hina and Swati chuckle, so he began.

'Once upon a time, there was a little boy, whom his mother loved a lot. But he never listened to her and never told her that he loved her too. One day, some monsters came and took her away, and the boy was all alone.'

Abhi took his hand and said, 'Just like my mama.'

'But then the boy had to be very brave because so many others needed him to be strong. So he decided that wherever his mama was, she would be proud if he didn't cry and was brave.'

He struggled with what to say next, feeling his throat tighten with tears. Fortunately, he didn't need to continue, because Abhi was falling asleep, his little chest rising and falling rhythmically.

Mayukh put Abhi's head on a cushion and sat down nearby, tears coming freely. He felt a hand on his shoulder. It was Swati.

'I thought the boy was going to be brave.'

Mayukh put his head against her shoulder and cried, and she just let him sit there, the two of them thinking of families they had lost, and of the uncertainties ahead.

Mayukh didn't realise when he dozed off, and when he awoke, the glowing hands of his watch told him it was three in the morning. Swati was fast asleep just inches from him.

He took out his mobile phone and turned it on. It was useless as a phone, but in the glow of its screen he took a look around the room. Hina was sleeping next to Abhi, a hand over his chest, and David still seemed to be outside. He then moved the glow over Swati's face. Her cheeks were streaked with dried tears that she herself must have shed after Mayukh slept. There was a swollen bruise on her forehead, but despite that, Mayukh thought she was the most beautiful girl he had ever seen. He would have loved to linger on her face, but she stirred in her sleep, and he hastily shut the phone off and lay down.

He had lapsed into an uneasy slumber when a tap on his shoulder woke him up. It was David.

'Come on, you have to see this.'

He followed David out, crouching low and then taking cover behind the podium outside the door. What he saw shocked him.

In the pale moonlight, five men were standing just a hundred metres from the bookstore. At any other time, they may have passed for a group of friends just shooting the breeze, but at this unearthly hour, and with their black turbans, there was no doubt who they were.

'David, do you think they know we're here?'

David asked him to crouch lower.

'I don't know how they did it, but they found us. We can smell their stench from here; maybe they can smell us as well. A few minutes ago there were just two of them.'

As he spoke, one of the men waved to someone in the distance. Four more figures joined the group. They made no move to attack the bookstore, but just stood there, watching and waiting. A few minutes later, six more joined the group.

One of them pointed straight towards the bookstore. Mayukh could not hear what was being said, but the group moved together towards the bookstore.

Mayukh turned to David. 'What the hell is going on?'

In the moonlight, he could just make out David's face, and the soldier's eyes seemed to betray a hint of uncertainty.

'They're learning ... I saw the same thing in Pakistan. They're getting better at communicating and coordinating. Go and see if any of them are at the back door.'

Mayukh scrambled to the back of the store, and after moving some of the furniture wedged against it, peeked outside the door. He heaved a sigh of relief when he saw nobody outside. He was about to go to the front entrance and pass on the good news to David when he heard the first gunshot.

When the figures began running towards the bookstore, David knew he had to do something. His assault rifle was resting against the top of the podium, and with the night vision scope on, he had a clear field of fire. While he was an excellent shot, it was still hard to hit moving targets, especially when the only shots that counted were ones to the head. So he emptied his magazine and was rewarded with four head shots which put his targets down on the ground.

The others continued running towards him.

David picked up his Claymore anti-personnel mine, placed it a few feet inside the door, and activated it. He picked up his gun and retreated inside the store, closing the door behind him, just as Mayukh reached him. The two of them piled shelves and tables against the door to barricade themselves in. The sounds had awakened Hina and Swati, who came up, asking what was going on.

'*They* are coming,' Mayukh said.

In a split second, Hina and Swati were helping to move furniture against the door. Mayukh glanced at Abhi to see that the boy was somehow managing to sleep through all the chaos.

Then the banging on the door began. First, it was the hammering of a single fist, and then it was joined by a multitude of others as the door shook and threatened to give way.

David was crouched in front of the door, his assault rifle at the ready. Mayukh stood a foot behind him, his handgun raised in his shaking hands.

As the door began to give way under the onslaught, David cried out, 'Get back and take cover behind something!'

Mayukh went to hide behind a bookshelf. He found Swati there, holding Abhi, who was awake now and sobbing.

The boy sensed Mayukh nearby and stammered, 'Are they the bad men? I'm scared.'

Abhi's plea put a new resolve in Mayukh. Whatever happened, the monsters outside the door would not get to Abhi as long as he was around. Somehow, it felt as if his destiny was to protect this little boy who trusted him so much. He aimed his gun at the door.

The door burst open under the constant hammering of the creatures outside.

The Claymore exploded with a deafening roar, sending

hundreds of pellets in a deadly arc, slicing through the first few creatures that came through the door.

The prone figures did not get back up, but in their place, many more were clambering in through the open door.

A flashlight suddenly turned on. David had just illuminated their targets. The two creatures in front seemed to flinch at the sudden explosion of light, and were trying to cover their eyes with their yellowed and bleeding hands when David fired.

Mayukh joined in, firing again and again, aiming for their heads. He had no idea if he was hitting anyone, but he continued to pull the trigger, Before he knew it, he heard the clicking noise indicating his magazine was empty. As he put another clip in the gun, David kept up a withering fire. Four more of their attackers lay in the doorway, but others climbed over their prone bodies and entered the store.

'Back!'

On David's command, Mayukh pulled Swati and Abhi towards the rear of the store, firing as he went. He saw one or two of the creatures stumble, but he knew that if he didn't hit their heads, he would not stop them, and even if he did, it was a matter of minutes before they would resume their attack. They were fighting a losing battle, and Mayukh and David both realised it.

A flashlight was now rolling on the floor, casting eerie shadows on the wall. David brought the butt of his rifle down hard on the head of one attacker before he too retreated into the store. Hina was screaming nearby, but in the darkness, he had no idea where she was.

Mayukh felt along the bookshelf behind him till he found Swati's hand. She gripped his hand tightly and whispered to Abhi, telling him that they were playing hide-and-seek. He couldn't see the boy in the darkness, but was amazed at how well he was holding up.

He could hear feet shuffling in the darkness as more of *them* entered the bookstore. He almost screamed when he felt a hand touching his shoulder.

'It's me, David. Try and get everyone to the back of the store and out that door.'

Mayukh felt David and Hina brush past him, and he leaned down to whisper to Swati what the plan was. Swati was about to move back when Mayukh felt Abhi hold his hand. He whispered to him to follow his sister, but the boy would not let go.

'I'm only going with you.'

Mayukh tried to hush him, but it was too late. There was an inhuman growl as their pursuers realised where they were. Mayukh spoke to Swati in a whisper.

'Move to the back of the store. Abhi and I will be right behind.'

Holding the boy's hand in his left hand, Mayukh took out his gun and crept along the bookshelf.

Behind him, one bookshelf after another fell in the darkness as their attackers trashed them in their hunt for their targets. When the first bookshelf fell with a resounding crash, Mayukh nearly jumped. The other bookshelves falling, some crashing into each other created an eerie crescendo and Mayukh could hear Abhi scream out in fright.

There was something cold and clammy against his right

hand. Mayukh let go of Abhi's hand and brought up his flashlight to see what it was.

He was looking into a yellowed, bloody face with a turban tied on top of its head. He seemed to be as surprised as Mayukh. He took a step back before baring his deformed teeth and emitting a howl that sounded like an animal in pain more than anything a human being could produce.

'Jiiiiiiiiiiiihaaaaaaaaaa...'

Without conscious thought, Mayukh brought up his gun and fired twice into the creature's face. He went down.

Any pretence of stealth was now useless.

'Abhi, can you be a brave boy and keep the flashlight pointed straight?'

The boy's eyes were wide with fear, but he nodded and said, 'Don't worry. I'll help you fight the monsters.'

Mayukh's heart went out to the brave little boy as he gave him the flashlight. He grabbed Abhi's hand and ran towards the back exit as footsteps sounded behind him. He turned in mid-stride, firing two shots into the darkness, not sure if he would hit anyone, but hoping to at least slow down their pursuers.

He was wrong. Having sensed prey, their attackers were crazed like a pack of wild dogs, rampaging through the store with a senseless fury, overturning bookshelves and ripping books to shreds.

Mayukh's shoulder slammed into the corner of a bookshelf. Ignoring the stinging pain, he dragged Abhi along as fast as he could. He could hear Swati screaming now for her brother, and as he got closer, he saw Swati, Hina and David silhouetted against the open back door.

David knelt down. Through the night vision optics of his assault rifle, focused on two of the creatures just behind Mayukh. He fired a single shot at each, the bullets whizzing inches past Mayukh's face as they slammed into his pursuer's heads. Both went down in a heap.

Mayukh stumbled on a book and fell forward. Even as he went down, he tried to cushion Abhi's fall with his body.

'You okay?'

'I'm still brave.'

Despite the danger they were in, Mayukh couldn't help but smile at the boy's innocent courage as he got up and started for the door again.

That was when a hand clamped around Abhi's left leg.

'He's got me!'

Abhi's shout was echoed by a scream of dismay from Swati. Mayukh picked up the flashlight the boy had dropped and shone it down.

He saw what had once been a young woman, but was now no more than a feral animal. Her right hand was holding Abhi's leg and she was opening her mouth to bite into it.

Mayukh fired at her, hitting her several times till his gun clicked empty.

She fell but, in a second, was about to get back up when Mayukh lifted Abhi in his arms and ran towards the door. As he reached it, David stepped forward, kneeling to fire his rifle on full auto at the woman, sending her down again.

They ran out the door and sprinted down the spiral staircase, David bringing up the rear.

Mayukh skidded to a stop. In front of them stood at least

a dozen of the infected, no more than twenty feet away. They began to wail, a sound that struck terror into Mayukh.

'Jiiiiiiihaaaaaaaaaaad...'

He pointed his gun at the nearest one and fired. His clip was empty. David came up next to him, his rifle at his shoulders.

'Shit, they are learning faster than I thought. They knew we'd come out here.'

Swati was gripping Mayukh's left hand and holding Abhi behind her.

David took a deep breath, inserted a fresh magazine into his rifle, and selected full auto. At this range, he had no hope of stopping all of them, but maybe he could buy some time for the others to get away. Iraq, Afghanistan, Yemen—he had survived all of them, only to die in a parking lot in Delhi. He took a step forward towards the wailing creatures.

'Folks, run to the front and get our car. I'll try and hold them off.'

Abhi was crying, all his courage gone. Swati tried to reach out to Mayukh, but he stepped away. 'Go!' he shouted at Swati and Hina, and stood next to David.

'You're the man next to me now, David. Remember what you told me?'

David grinned. In another life, this kid could have been a good soldier.

'Nice knowing you, kid. Let's give 'em hell.'

When the creatures saw Hina, Swati and Abhi run, they screamed and thundered down on them in pursuit. With Mayukh and David standing in their way, they would have to get past them first. David knelt and emptied his magazine, sending four of them tumbling to the ground. Mayukh was firing as fast as he could, and thought he hit two of them, there was no time to check. He put in another clip as David fired again.

Their attackers were now just feet away from them and Mayukh put his gun down, knowing that the end was near. David was still firing and shouting obscenities at the creatures.

Mayukh flinched as the nearest attacker launched himself at him, teeth bared. That was when the SUV ploughed into them, scattering their attackers and running over two of them. Hina was at the wheel.

'Get in!'

Mayukh and David dived through the open back door as Hina sped away, smashing aside a bike that was parked near the exit. She glanced at them in the rear view mirror and said, 'Did I tell you that I never got a driver's license because I was scared of driving?'

There was a cry of anguish from Abhi, and they all turned towards him, wondering what was wrong. The little boy looked at Mayukh, tears in his eyes.

'I left McQueen in there.'

They laughed and sat back, each of them thinking of their narrow escape.

As the sun slowly rose over the city, they realised they had survived one more night. Not just survived, but formed the kind of bonds forged in battle. Now each of them knew that, no matter what lay ahead, they would face it together.

'Oh my god!'

Mayukh sat up at Swati's words, as she began to cry. She was cradling Abhi in her lap, and was looking at his left leg.

'Swati, what happened?'

'They bit Abhi.'

SIX

They were sitting inside Haldiram's. Though they were starving and exhausted, food was the last thing on their minds. Abhi was in front of them, scratching his left leg near the knee, his expression showing just how confused he was at how the adults were behaving. Unconsciously, all of them, even Swati, were sitting a couple of feet away from Abhi. They could see the red welt where one of the creatures had sunk its teeth. It had not been a deep bite, but the skin had broken and there was some bleeding.

'It hurts here,' he said with a pout, puzzled why he was not getting more sympathy.

Mayukh felt gutted; guilty for not having taken better care of Abhi. There was a knot in his stomach. Once again, he had let someone who had depended on him down.

Hina was trying to console Swati, who was in tears, while David sat impassively, cradling his rifle in his hands. He was the first to break the silence.

'It's been at least two hours since he was bitten. How long do we wait?'

David moved the rifle in his hand.

Mayukh walked over and sat with Abhi, taking him in his lap. Abhi hugged him, grateful that finally someone was acting normal.

'David, we keep waiting. If anyone is worried, they can leave.'

Swati came and sat next to Mayukh, and a moment later, Hina walked over to them.

David put his rifle down on the ground in horror.

'Jesus, folks, don't be so frigging melodramatic. What did you think ...?'

He couldn't bring himself to say it, but he gestured towards his rifle, making his meaning obvious, and then continued.

'But look, he should have turned into one of them by now, and he hasn't. I don't understand it, and it freaks me out. And if he does turn into one of those things, what do you propose we do?'

They were silent. None of them had an answer to that question which had been plaguing their minds for the past few hours.

Hina got up and walked to the kitchen.

'Look, we can sit around and wait, or we could at least get something to eat. Now, who wants cold dosas?'

The dosas were not just cold, but also stale, so they all gave it a pass, instead gorging on some packed sweets and ready-to-eat meals they found. The restaurant seemed to have been looted, but there were still more than enough packaged sweets and snacks around for them.

David discovered that the restaurant had a working generator, and they had their first hot meal in three days. It made them all feel a bit more human again, and it took their minds off Abhi.

While Hina sang nursery rhymes to Abhi, Mayukh decided

to stretch his legs and walked to the front of the restaurant. He felt someone come up behind him—it was Swati.

'The little boy's mother would have been really proud, for her little boy is a man.'

He looked at her and smiled.

'Tell me about your family,' he said.

Swati shrugged. 'We were hardly a perfect family. My parents fought all the time, so it was pretty much me and Abhi. And with our age difference, I guess I became part-mother, part-sister for him.'

She paused, and then continued, almost in a whisper, 'When *they* came to our house ... I ... I saw my dad run away. He didn't even try and protect us ...'

She was beginning to cry. Mayukh put his hand tentatively on her shoulder. She leaned against his chest and the tears now flowed freely.

Hina looked at the two of them and she smiled in the middle of singing 'London Bridge is falling down'. David, who had laid his weapons out in front of him and was cleaning his guns and taking stock of how much ammunition he had left, followed Hina's gaze.

Shaking his head, he said, 'I know what you're thinking Hina. You're obviously a born romantic.'

Hina looked at him and mockingly chided him.

'Young man, I have been writing trashy romance novels since when you were in diapers. I know a budding romance when I see one.'

She added a bit wistfully. 'At least there are some beautiful things still left in this world.'

Another hour passed. The roads outside were still deserted,

and as before, there was no sign of the infected in daylight. Abhi continued to be his normal self, and after much effort, Swati was finally able to make him take a nap.

With Abhi finally unable to hear them, the adults converged near the front door to talk about him. Swati was visibly relieved to see that her little brother had not changed. David was just happy he'd not had to figure out what to do with an infected toddler.

'I just don't get it. We've seen people of all ages, genders, religions transform after being bitten or scratched by *them*. If anything, the process of infection has gotten faster—it's nearly instantaneous now. Yet, there he is, sleeping away as if nothing had happened.'

'I'm just glad he's okay. I don't care why or how this happened; I'm just glad that he's fine.'

Mayukh's relief was born not just out of the affection he had begun to feel for the boy who followed him around like a lost puppy, but also because he didn't know if he could have lived with himself if anything had happened to Abhi when he was supposed to be taking care of him.

There was a silence before Hina spoke up, her soft words taking everyone aback: 'Perhaps it's a sign.'

When everyone looked at her to see what she meant, she continued.

'I've never been very religious, but don't tell me the scientists can fully explain what happened. In the middle of all this evil, all this chaos, Abhi not getting infected is a sign that there is hope. Maybe there is a way this infection can be beaten, and Swati, maybe your brother could be the key.'

They stood there, watching Abhi sleep, wondering how

true Hina's words were. Just then, he woke up, and called out to Mayukh.

'Can we play hide-and-seek now?'

The day had passed well enough, but by three in the afternoon, David began to wonder what their next step should be. Mayukh, finally tired from playing with the indefatigable Abhi, came over and sat next to him.

David looked at him; it seemed, somehow, that Mayukh's face was different from what it had been just a day earlier. Gone was the scared, shaken boy, and in its place was a young man who was not just capable of killing, but was prepared to get killed to protect those around him. David touched him on the shoulder.

'I never got around to telling you, but you did good this morning.'

Mayukh smiled at the compliment.

'Yeah, but I was shit scared all the time.'

David chuckled, but his eyes were serious.

'I'm still terrified every time I get into a firefight. I'd be worried if you *weren't* scared. What makes us do what we do as soldiers is not about being fearless, but putting something above that fear—honour, watching out for our buddies ... whatever works for each person. For you, I suspect it's our new friends there.'

Mayukh nodded. 'I've never been around kids much, but Abhi is amazing. I really feel like I'd do anything for him.'

David got up to stretch and told Mayukh he was going inside for a bio break, but then turned around and said with a wink, 'I wasn't just talking about the boy, and you know that.'

Mayukh reddened a bit. He was watching the road when Swati came up and joined him.

'Now I know what they say about grandmothers is true. Hina's spoiling him silly—he's drinking Pepsi. I never let him drink soda.'

Mayukh watched her, wondering just how true David's observation was. It sounded absurd—in the middle of all this chaos, where just staying alive was a constant struggle, who had time to be interested in a girl?

A sudden scraping noise somewhere outside the door caught Mayukh's attention. He whispered to Swati to get David and then braced himself against the door, his gun in hand.

As the sound got closer, Mayukh realised that it sounded like someone was dragging something along, but now it was joined by another noise, which sounded incongruously like glasses being clinked together.

Mayukh tried to control his breathing and calm himself. He thought of all the lessons his father had given him on the range, about how calm breathing was the key to a steady hand while taking a shot, and tried reminding himself that he had already seen more than enough action over the last two days. Yet, he couldn't help it—his hands seemed to shake of their own accord. He gripped his gun with both hands and then when the sound outside seemed very close, he braced himself for action.

Abruptly, the sound stopped. A raspy voice spoke just outside the door, perhaps inches from where his face was.

'You can relax and put your gun down. I mean no harm.'

Mayukh was puzzled: how did the stranger know he was

there, and that he had his gun at the ready? David came up beside him and swung open the door, pointing his assault rifle straight at the man outside. Mayukh joined him a second later and found himself facing an old, bespectacled man.

The man was thin and wore tweed trousers and a pullover. He would have looked like someone's grandfather out for a walk, had it not been for two things. He wore a thick belt around his waist on which were tied several beer bottles, with a rag stuffed at the end of each. His right leg was bent at a strange angle, and he dragged it behind him as he walked.

'How did you know I was there?' asked Mayukh.

The man smiled and held out an old, gnarled hand to Mayukh and then to David, sizing up the American soldier, and noticing the insignia on his arm.

'I didn't expect to see a SEAL here. Gentlemen, I am Lieutenant General Purohit, Indian Army. I retired ten years ago, but I spent most of my career as a commando in the Paras, and I had the good fortune to train with some of your SEAL comrades. Young man, as for how I knew you were there—I could see a bit of your shadow outside the door. You're lucky I waited to see who you were before doing anything.'

Mayukh saw the pistol tucked into the old man's belt and knew he'd had a narrow escape. When David saluted the man to introduce himself, the old soldier's back straightened as he saluted back. They welcomed him in and introductions were made.

'I'm really glad to see some more survivors,' he said as he sat down, taking off the small backpack he had been carrying.

Hina gave him a cup of tea that he gratefully accepted, and for the next few minutes, they told him how they had got there. It was the first time they had really heard each other's stories, and Mayukh realised just how different each of them was. David, the soldier trying to get home; Hina, the lonely woman who didn't know how her family was doing; Swati and Abhi, abandoned by their father, and now on their own; and of course himself. All thrown together by the chaos, and now, despite their very different backgrounds, a team.

David addressed Purohit. 'Sir, if you don't mind me asking, how did you get away and what happened to you?'

The old man took a long sip of his tea before answering.

'They came for us on the first night. Our kids all live abroad, so it was just Asha and me, reading and watching TV as usual, our routine after forty years of marriage. I was drinking my daily glass of Scotch. The monsters got her as they came in. She was a soldier's wife and fought like a tigress, so they ...'

He paused, as if trying to come to grips with what had happened, and Hina held his left hand for support. He took it gratefully as he continued.

'Then the first bastard came for me. I am old, but I was a Para, and I wanted to make them pay for what they did to Asha, so I kicked the bugger and as he fell, I ran into the kitchen to find something to fight them with. I threw oil into the entrance to the kitchen and set it on fire to slow them down, and then I learnt something that helped me live.'

Just then a voice crackled in his backpack. He reached in, took out a walkie-talkie, and spoke into it.

'Bartender here. Over.'

'Bartender, Margarita here. Sector two is clear. Am on the way back to HQ. Over.'

'Roger, Margarita. Other cocktails acknowledge and report in before sunset. Over.'

'Tequila, over and out.'

'Screwdriver, over and out.'

Everyone looked at him with a mixture of awe and curiosity. Finally, David said, 'Sir, you seem to have some sort of organised operation going on here. Do you mind sharing what you've learnt and what you're doing?'

Purohit laughed.

'Operation! We're just a bunch of old fogies playing soldier all over again. I and my cocktails—three old army buddies who were having a drink in the next building when the shit hit the fan.'

But then his face turned serious. 'We all lost families and loved ones to those monsters. We're old and retired but we were all soldiers once, and when someone messes with our families, we fight back. That's all we're trying to do now.'

'But sir, these creatures can't be killed. I've shot dozens of them at point-blank range, and even a shot in their head puts them down for only a minute. How can we fight back?'

Purohit smiled grimly.

'Son, everything can be killed. We just need to know how. Now, it's almost dark, and I wouldn't recommend your staying here on the main road. Join us for the night and we can talk more.'

They followed Purohit through narrow alleys till they reached a section of old shop-houses approached only by a single walkway. They walked up a flight of stairs to a second-floor apartment. Inside it were three men, all wearing belts with a couple of bottles hung from them, and armed with handguns. They nodded at the newcomers as Purohit told them briefly how he had chanced upon them. It was clear that Purohit was the one in charge, since the others didn't question his decision of bringing strangers back even once.

Purohit looked outside the window and said in a whisper, 'The sun's going down. Get ready.'

The men, each at least seventy years old, moved with the precision of a military unit. Lamps were snuffed out, till only a single kerosene lamp was left burning on the floor. Screwdriver and Tequila went downstairs to stand vigil while Margarita, who was bald, moved to the other room. Purohit asked everyone to sit down and make themselves comfortable.

'I'm afraid I can't offer much hospitality. We found this two-room affair a day ago—small but very defensible. Also, I'm afraid we may not have much to make the little one comfortable, but you'll be safe here.'

Abhi was nestled between Mayukh and Swati. Mayukh marvelled at just how much the boy had adapted. After their escape from the bookstore, there had been no diapers or milk, but as if sensing the situation they were in, he had not complained once, and when he had needed to go to the bathroom, had told Swati, who had muttered, 'So, all we needed to do to toilet-train this brat was to bring about the end of the world as we know it!'

'Why does Uncle carry bottles?' Abhi asked now. 'Are you very thirsty?'

Purohit laughed. 'Yes, son, I do like to drink. And I like to mix drinks, which is why my old friends call me Bartender.'

His curiosity satisfied, Abhi proceeded to walk through the small apartment, and emitted a squeal of delight when he found a small book in a corner. He ran back to Mayukh, his eyes gleaming.

'I got Bob!'

Mayukh looked towards Swati for help. She smiled indulgently at Abhi.

'Since he's adopted you as a guardian, you should really brush up on kid's movies and books. That's from Bob the Builder, a cartoon on the Disney Channel.'

Mayukh had never seen the show, but played along with Abhi, reading the book till the boy tired and went to sleep on Hina's lap.

Hina whispered to everyone, 'It's amazing what one child can do. With him around, it doesn't feel like we're living from one day to another.'

Finally, Mayukh asked Purohit how he thought the creatures could be killed. Purohit unslung a bottle from his belt.

'The word is Biters.'

'What?'

'That's what they're being called by everyone.'

'Everyone?' David asked. 'You mean there are others like us out there?'

Purohit nodded. 'There are hundreds in this neighbourhood alone. People just hunkering down and hiding, too scared to come out at night or day. And then there are those taking advantage of the situation: gangs raping and looting at will.

What those damn Biters won't do, we'll do ourselves to finish it all off.'

Hina lay Abhi down on a pillow and came over.

'So there is hope that at some point this will go away?'

'I wouldn't go that far. As you've seen yourself, the Biters are learning and evolving as well. They don't yet act with any cohesion, but the moment they do, it will be a whole new nightmare.'

Mayukh felt a hand slide into his in the darkness. He pressed Swati's hand and held it as Purohit continued.

'I'm called the Bartender because I found out that one way to kill the Biters is through fire. That's why I and my friends have these Molotov cocktails with us at all times.'

A voice called out through his walkie-talkie.

'Margarita here. The Biters are coming!'

Hina moved Abhi to the second room, which was away from the street, and David took up position at the window, saying that with his night vision optics, he'd be in a better position to spot any intruders. Mayukh was about to go to the stairwell when Purohit called out to him.

'Just stay in the second room.'

Without turning to face Purohit, David said, 'Mayukh's part of my squad. He can take care of himself. Let him stand guard at the stairwell.'

Purohit nodded and came up to Mayukh and handed him a bottle and a lighter.

'It's simple enough. Light the cloth at the end and throw it.

Just remember to let go within three seconds or so, otherwise you'll be the one fried.'

Mayukh saw that Screwdriver and Tequila were also crouched in the stairwell while Margarita was downstairs at the doorway. He suddenly called out. 'The Biters found the family hiding next door!'

'I told them to join us or to move away, but that stubborn old man wouldn't listen.'

Mayukh could hear the anguish in Purohit's voice.

The screams were bloodcurdling but mercifully brief as Margarita ran up the stairs, much faster than Mayukh would have expected an old, overweight man to move.

'They're here!'

Mayukh saw several shadows crowding the doorway, but before any of them could even get in the door, one of the men next to him lit his Molotov and threw it straight through the open door. The bottle smashed against the ground, spewing the kerosene around in a growing inferno. With high-pitched screams, the Biters scattered.

They continued to hear sounds of carnage from nearby houses, but there was no further attempt to come into their hideout. Clearly, the Biters had figured that opposition in this particular house was particularly virulent.

Mayukh watched the fire flicker outside the door, and saw a body engulfed in flames. As the fire consumed the body, it seemed to collapse upon itself and dissolve into ashes.

David called out, 'They seem to be leaving for now.'

They kept up an uneasy watch through the night. After a couple of hours, Mayukh went to the second room to see how the others were doing.

Abhi was fast asleep, with Hina next to him. Swati was lying in a corner, but sat up when Mayukh walked in.

'Hey, it's just me.'

As he sat down, she moved next to him and he took her hand. His hands were shaking and she held them tight. Her head was on his shoulder and as Mayukh turned to say something to her, his face brushed hers. He could now feel her breath on his face, and he paused. What was he doing?

They continued to sit next to each other. It was immensely comforting to simply know that they were not alone, that they had someone they could turn to for support. Mayukh leaned over and kissed her. A tentative first kiss, but when he reached over and kissed her again, she kissed him back.

Mayukh whispered, 'You do realise I haven't brushed my teeth in three days?'

'Neither have I,' Swati murmured back. 'Since one kiss hasn't killed either of us, I guess we should be okay for more.'

They sat holding each other till dawn broke.

Mayukh had just washed his face and was walking out of the bathroom, when he bumped into Hina.

'You two make a good couple.'

Mayukh started to protest, especially when he saw that Swati was within earshot.

'Hina, don't let your novelist's imagination get the better of you.'

'You know, I wasn't as fast asleep as you may have thought last night.'

Swati reddened. Mayukh walked quickly to the other room, mumbling something about having to talk to David, leaving Hina cackling in delight.

He found David and Purohit in a huddle. Purohit had a small box in his hand, and he seemed to be cranking a handle. He held the box up to the window, but all that came out of it was the hiss of static.

'We'll try again later, David. You never know when the damn thing will speak again.'

'I wonder if anyone is left out there. My tactical radio hasn't picked up anything other than some recorded message saying we should stand by for orders.'

Mayukh sat down next to them and asked them what they were doing. Purohit answered as he put the box inside a duffel bag, 'I have an old radio and David has a new fancy one in his backpack—but the result is the same. We were trying to see if anyone's transmitting, but so far it's all quiet out there.'

'What's your plan for today?'

Purohit answered David with a shrug as he got up to put on his belt with the Molotov cocktails hanging from it.

'The usual routine. We'll fan out and look for other survivors and pass on the word about how to kill the Biters and see if we can get a bit more organised in our defence. The problem is most people are too scared to worry about fighting back. Then we scrounge for food and drink.'

David, conscious that they had doubled the number of mouths Purohit had to feed, told him about all the supplies they had left behind at the bookstore. They quickly agreed that David and one more man would go out in the SUV to pick up whatever they could find at the bookstore. Mayukh said that he would go along with David.

'You said you'd tell me a story about the brave boy again!'

Abhi, refreshed after his sleep and on a sugar high after a chocolate-bar breakfast, bounded into the room and landed on Mayukh's lap with a jump that would have done an Olympic athlete proud. Then he grimaced in pain.

'What happened, Abhi?'

'I hurt myself.'

Abhi lifted his leg to show Purohit where the bite mark was still visible.

'Abhi, how did that happen?'

As Abhi started to respond, David cut in. 'He fell down while we were on the run.'

Hina and Swati were now in the room, and Mayukh could see the growing fear on Swati's face as Purohit signalled with one hand for David to be quiet.

'Let the boy answer, David. So Abhi, what happened to your leg?'

Abhi, playfully tugging at Mayukh's shoelaces, answered innocently. 'One of those not-nice uncles bit me. They were chasing us, and then we shot them. Bang! Bang!'

A sudden silence descended over the room. Mayukh could feel the tension in Purohit's voice as he stood up and took a step back. Mayukh sensed the other three old men standing behind him, and he heard the unmistakable sound of a gun being cocked.

'Purohit, have you lost your mind?'

David was on his feet and reaching for his rifle, when Mayukh saw that Purohit had raised his pistol.

'David, please don't. I don't doubt you could kill me even if I got a shot in, but you won't be able to take all four of us. Why didn't you tell me this boy was bitten by one of the Biters?'

Mayukh stood up and advanced towards Purohit. He had his own gun drawn.

'Look, let Abhi and the others move to the other room and we can talk.'

Purohit tried to raise his voice. 'That boy ...' But he couldn't finish his sentence.

Mayukh roared with an anger he had never known himself to be capable of, 'That boy is in my care, and if you even think about touching him, nobody here will walk away alive! So calm the hell down and listen to us!'

Purohit nodded and lowered his gun. Swati and Abhi moved to the other room, but stayed by the door so they could hear everything as Mayukh told the men how Abhi had been bitten but was not infected.

Purohit put his gun aside and sat down.

'I'm sorry. After all that's happened, I didn't want to risk one of us turning into a Biter. But this is unbelievable. The boy must be the first person ever to have been bitten but not infected.'

Nervous at the sudden attention he was getting, Abhi ran to Mayukh and hid himself behind him.

Purohit reached out and tousled his hair. 'Abhi, do you want another chocolate?'

Abhi's face lit up, all the anxiety gone, and he wolfed down the chocolate bar that Purohit handed him.

As Mayukh and David were about to leave for the bookstore,

Mayukh quietly handed his gun to Swati. 'Keep it in case you have to use it.'

The trip to the bookstore was uneventful, and David and Mayukh were thrilled to find that their food and supplies were largely untouched, including Abhi's diapers and formula. They loaded them into the SUV, and as they drove back, they began to see more signs of people. A young couple peering out from a window; two young men armed with cricket bats roaming the streets; a family foraging for food in the remains of a restaurant. The initial terror had given way to thoughts of survival, and people were coming out in the daytime to look for food and supplies. And also to prey on others.

Mayukh saw three men on bikes ride up to the young couple's hideout. A gun blazed and the man inside fell. The three men started to pull the woman out. Mayukh felt for the gun at his belt and remembered he had given it to Swati. He turned and saw a glint in David's eye, a look that would have frightened any man.

'Those bastards! After all that's happened, one would think we'd learn to help each other.'

As the woman tried in vain to hold off her attackers, David stopped the SUV and put his rifle to his shoulder, selecting single-shot mode. One assailant fell to the ground moaning in pain as a bullet slammed into his thigh. Another twirled around and fell against the window, as a bullet caught him in the shoulder. The third, seeing his friends fall to an unseen attacker, ran to his bike. He never made it, a single bullet catching him in the knee.

David drove on in silence till they reached Purohit's

headquarters. It was four in the afternoon, and they had to begin planning for the night that lay ahead.

Mayukh was shocked to see a crowd of at least twenty people gathered on the roadside. As they parked, one of them whispered to Mayukh, 'Have you also come to see the miracle boy?'

Wondering what was going on, Mayukh and David ran up the stairs, to find Purohit and his friends sitting at the stairwell, fully armed. Margarita had a bloody lip.

'What happened to you?' David asked.

'I hit him,' Purohit answered quietly, still watching the crowd outside. 'The fool met a group of survivors and told them about how Abhi had survived being bitten. The word's spread like wildfire—people think it's a miracle. Some of them are saying that if Abhi touches them, they'll be immune as well.'

'Oh shit! Why the hell did you do that?'

The man whom Mayukh had heard referred to only as Margarita averted his eyes.

'Everyone has given up. They're just waiting to die. Don't you get it? Abhi gives them, gives all of us, some hope. But maybe I should have kept my mouth shut.'

Purohit leaned out the window and shouted, 'People, there's no miracle boy here. It's almost sunset anyway. Get the hell back to wherever you're hiding before the Biters come. Good luck.'

At the mention of the Biters, the crowd melted away, but Mayukh knew that they would have to find another hideout soon.

Purohit and his friends helped carry the supplies in, and

they settled down to an early dinner just as the sun began to set. When they were finished, Purohit tried his luck with his radio again. At first there was only the familiar static, but then suddenly they all heard a voice.

'All is not lost. Survivors are regrouping across the world. If you're anywhere in northern India, come to Ladakh if you can. We are army soldiers and are based at the Thirse Monastery. You will be safe here.'

After a few seconds, the announcement was repeated once, and then there was nothing but static. They all looked at each other, stunned at the announcement they had just heard.

Then the Biters began screaming outside.

SEVEN

'THEY'RE UP early tonight,' said Purohit as he quickly snuffed out all the lamps and took up vigil near the window. David was right beside him.

It was just after sunset, and he had no real need of the night vision scope to see what was happening outside. There were more than two dozen Biters gathered at the mouth of the alley leading to the apartment, just standing there and screaming incoherently. Abhi had begun sobbing at the noise, and Hina took him into the other room, trying in vain to distract him.

'Why are they just standing there?'

There was no ready answer to Swati's question and David shrugged, lowering his rifle for a moment.

'No idea whatsoever, but let's not assume they even know we're here. I think they may be able to smell or sense us, but I don't know for sure. Maybe they'll just scream and leave us alone.'

Mayukh wasn't so sure, and guessed that David was trying to reassure Swati more than anything else. The Biters had shown some level of coordination and thinking during the battle at the bookstore, and if it was true that they were beginning to learn and evolve, there was no telling what would come next.

The three men with Purohit were huddled in the stairwell,

a bottle in each hand, waiting for the order to launch their deadly cocktails. David looked at the Biters through his scope, seeing the outlines of the deformed faces and the telltale turbans on their heads.

'Wonder what's with the damned turbans?'

Purohit sniggered.

'Damned Taliban jihadis in Afghanistan started it all. Or at least that's what the news said. Maybe it's something that's still in their memory and transmitted along with the infection.'

David took in the information in silence, thinking back to his own tour of duty in Afghanistan and the carnage at his base.

A thought came to Mayukh.

'If that memory stayed with them and is somehow being transmitted to anyone infected, what other memories could they have? Maybe they aren't learning new skills—they're just remembering things they knew.'

Just then, the group of Biters began moving along the alley as one, their feet making a dull thumping sound on the pavement. They stopped when they were just ten metres away; none of them were screaming now. Mayukh held his breath as he desperately hoped that perhaps they didn't have a particular target in mind, maybe they would just pass by.

That was when one of the Biters stepped forward, raised his right hand and pointed straight at the window where Mayukh, David and Purohit were huddled. He uttered an ululating scream.

'Kaaaaaaaaaaaaaaaaaaaaaaaaaaffffffrrrrrr.'

David felled him with a single bullet between the eyes, as

the other Biters rushed towards the apartment. Purohit lit one bottle and flung it, the bottle bouncing off the far wall, and creating a sheet of flame that enveloped two of the Biters who went down screeching in agony, and were reduced to ashes in seconds. Margarita lit one of his bottles and advanced down the stairs, cocking his arm back to throw it towards the Biters who were now about to enter the stairwell.

That was when something totally unexpected happened. Three of the Biters took out rocks they had been hiding behind them and flung them at the men in the stairwell. They were clumsy throws, with aim and force no better than if they had been flung by small children. Yet in the confined space, and since everyone was taken totally by surprise, they caused Margarita to stumble. The bottle fell near his feet, engulfing him in flames. He screamed and rolled down the stairs, as more stones followed, targeting the two remaining men. Tequila was hit in the forehead, and he slipped, falling down the stairs. Two Biters leaped over the burning man and tore into him, biting and clawing him till he was dead. Screwdriver, the remaining man guarding the stairwell, ran in utter terror up the stairs.

David and Purohit were now at the top of the winding stairs and David fired a series of well-aimed shots over the retreating man, hitting two Biters in the head. As they went down, Purohit launched one more Molotov cocktail, incinerating both of them and creating a barrier of flames that held the other Biters at bay.

It was now an uneasy standoff. There were still more than twenty Biters outside, and they were now standing flat against the wall, so that they could not be targeted from the window.

If they did all decide to rush the stairwell, David wasn't sure they would be able to hold them all off. He knew Purohit and friends scavenged every day for kerosene for their Molotov cocktails, and they would not have nearly enough to destroy such a large group.

Mayukh was watching out the window when he saw a shadow move to his left. He aimed and fired four rounds. The Biter was hit at least twice and fell, but staggered to his feet a few seconds later. That gave Mayukh the time to light a bottle, and as he felt the heat expand under his hand, he threw it. The bottle landed a mere foot in front of the Biter and he screamed as the fire took him. In the glow of the flames, Mayukh saw that the other Biters were now gathering near the door.

'David, they're going to rush the door!'

Help arrived from a totally unexpected quarter. From a rooftop across the alley, someone dumped a bucketful of oil down on the Biters, and then someone threw a lamp. The sudden explosion of light and fire caused Mayukh to flinch and take cover, and when he looked out the window again, several of the Biters were on fire, and the others were scattering.

From another rooftop, someone else threw two kerosene lanterns in their path, incinerating a couple more of them, as the remaining Biters escaped.

They didn't sleep a wink till the sun finally came out, wary of another assault, but the Biters seemed to have had enough for the night.

When the sun finally rose, Purohit slumped to the ground, looking like the frail old man he was, and no longer the tough commando on vigil. He had lost two good friends in the night, and Screwdriver was in a state of shock. David looked worried, and his expression mirrored what was on everyone's minds. The Biters had learnt how to use crude weapons, and moreover, they were not just attacking targets at random. The assault on their apartment had been a planned and coordinated one.

Mayukh and Swati held each other, trying hard to ignore the stench of burnt flesh that was wafting up from the stairwell. Abhi was clinging to Mayukh's leg, but he was able to offer no real comfort to the boy.

Only one person seemed to have retained some composure, and that was an unlikely candidate—Hina. She gently took Abhi from Mayukh and gave him some food, telling him that everyone was tired and needed rest.

'Will they play with me then?'

Hina assured him that they would, and then she approached Purohit, laying a hand on his shoulder. The old man looked up at her, trying hard to control his tears.

Suddenly several voices echoed in the alley below.

'Is the boy okay?'

They peered out the window to see more than a dozen men, women and children outside.

An old woman stepped forward and shouted in a hoarse voice, 'Get the boy to safety. The Biters know about him and will come again for him.'

These were the people who had helped defend them the previous night, Mayukh realised. Purohit and David leaned out and thanked everyone for their help and assured them that Abhi was fine.

Mayukh turned to Swati and saw that her face reflected the same panic he felt creeping up his spine. She spoke slowly, as if afraid that saying the words would somehow make them more real.

'The Biters can't be figuring things out, can they? They're just crazed with the infection, right?'

Mayukh would have liked to reassure her, but he had seen enough to tell him that the Biters were not just the bloodthirsty, random zombies they had initially seemed to be. There was surely a method to their madness, albeit a slowly developing one as if more elements of whatever collective memories or intentions had formed the original infection were coming back, beyond just a reflexive desire to wear a turban and attack others.

David was looking Mayukh straight in the eye, and Mayukh saw the soldier motion for him to come to a corner.

Swati said, 'David, I know you're going to talk about Abhi. Whatever it is, let's say it in the open.'

David sighed.

'Fair enough. We're all in this together now. Look, even if there is a slim chance that they are indeed trying to target Abhi, we all need to get out of here fast. We almost had it last night, and if they come in greater numbers, we don't stand a chance.'

Hina had been trying to keep Abhi busy in a corner, but the boy knew that they were all talking about him. He looked at David, growing fear in his eyes.

'Are those not-nice people coming to get me?'

Mayukh wanted to hold him tight and tell him that everything would be fine, but that kind of innocence and simplicity in his life was long gone, gone the night the infection began spreading, gone the moment his family had been shattered. He picked Abhi up and held him close. For several moments, there was an awkward silence as they all considered David's words.

Purohit broke the silence.

'I don't know whether they came for him or not, but the boy is the biggest threat to them, and the biggest hope for all of us. So he must be protected.'

Hina asked him what he meant.

'For whatever reason, he is immune to the infection. If scientists or doctors got a look at him, they may find out why, and be able to come up with a vaccine or cure for the infection.'

Despairingly, Mayukh said, 'Doctors? Scientists? All that's left are these goddamn Biters and people like us who are just trying to stay alive.'

Purohit shook his head.

'No, Mayukh. There is more than that—and it all starts with people regaining hope. You saw what happened last night. Total strangers, people who till now had just been hiding like rats, came out and fought to protect us. They did it because Abhi gives them hope that things can be better. We of all people cannot give up hope now.'

David nodded, and said in little more than a whisper, 'Mayukh, he's right. Don't you remember the radio transmission we heard yesterday?'

A flash of understanding came over Mayukh. They now had a destination.

Ladakh.

Their first stop was the bookstore, where they picked up maps and guides. When they learnt that the temperature could be near freezing at this time of the year, they went into a shop that once sold winter clothes. For a minute, they all stood there, looking at the jackets and sweaters strewn on the floor.

David spoke for all of them. 'Never thought we'd have to steal.'

Purohit scoffed. 'You're getting soft, soldier—you're trained to live off the land.'

They started picking up clothes and trying them on. Swati emerged from a changing room with a new sweater on.

'How do I look?'

Mayukh was about to say they had more pressing worries than to find clothes that looked good on them, but one look at Swati's face stopped him. She was smiling. This one simple activity of being in a shop, looking for clothes, had brought back memories of a normalcy that they had scarce little of in their lives now. Mayukh walked up to her and kissed her on her forehead.

'You look amazing.'

He could hear Abhi groan and he turned to see the boy sticking out his tongue.

'Yeeeeks ... he kissed her!'

The entire group burst out laughing, and they left the store in good spirits.

Next up was getting enough fuel for the ride. Delhi to Leh was a thousand-kilometre drive, and even in perfect weather, could take an experienced driver a full day of driving non-stop to get there, given the mountain passes and roads.

David, who had fought and lived in the cold, mountainous terrain of Afghanistan, knew what they would require.

'We'll need some metal cans to store the extra fuel. At high altitudes, plastic jerry cans will give out the smell of petrol, and together with the thin air, it's a recipe for throwing up. Any idea where we could get some of those?'

Mayukh thumbed through the guide in his hand.

'Sadar Bazaar.'

They drove in silence, looking at what remained of a once bustling city. Here and there people were wandering around in small groups, mostly scavenging for food or warm clothes. A frail woman with a toddler in her arms walked in front of the car, pleading for help.

Mayukh realised, not without a tinge of shame, that under normal circumstances, he ignored a dozen such beggars on the streets of Delhi every day. Somehow, with all that had happened, that did not seem right. He asked David to stop. Swati took a couple of packs of food and pressed them into the woman's hands. The woman thanked them, and then looked inside the SUV. She gazed at Mayukh with her vacant eyes, and leaned forward to whisper, 'Take care of the child. *They* are looking for him.'

Mayukh recoiled as if struck, and the woman scurried away. He didn't say anything to anyone, not wanting to spook Swati any further, but he clutched Abhi tightly to his chest. The stakes were now much more than just his personal survival.

At the best of times, Sadar Bazaar was a chaotic warren of shops, put together haphazardly as if a giant had taken them all, juggled them and then strewn them around at random. Now, with no lighting, and no signs of anyone around, the area looked positively creepy. Purohit and David went inside a shop to look for metal cans that might be useful. Mayukh stayed near the SUV, standing guard with Screwdriver. He'd finally learned the man's real name, Lamba. While they waited, Mayukh asked him what his story was.

'I was a Brigadier in the army before I retired. I served under Purohit sir for some years, but my health did not keep up with my plans.'

The man was wheezing slightly, and Mayukh thought about how hard it must have been for him to lose two of his friends in the fight the previous night.

Suddenly, he felt the hair on the back of his neck rise, and he had the uncanny feeling that he was being watched. He turned around to see an abandoned car repair shop that seemed completely shuttered, save for a small gap near the floor. He looked closely, and he could have sworn he saw a pair of eyes peering out.

Thinking it might be a frightened survivor, he went closer, his gun at the ready. He knelt down and looked through the gap. Whoever was inside had retreated into the darkness, but he thought he could hear breathing. Mayukh went even closer, and then the familiar stench hit him. He fell back, scrambling his way to the vehicle.

Purohit and David were back from the shop, and they asked him what had happened. When he told them, David simply took out his pistol.

'Only one way to find out.'

He fired a single shot through the hole, and they all heard

not one, but several of the unearthly shrieks that had come to haunt their nights. Everyone hurried inside the vehicle and they drove off.

Addressing no one in particular, Hina said, 'They hide during the day.'

It was now almost noon, and they knew they would have to stop somewhere before sunset. They briefly debated whether they should wait another night, but Swati insisted they push on.

'If *they* are really after Abhi, I want to get as far away as possible.'

They stopped at an abandoned petrol pump and took all the fuel they could carry. They took stock of their food and warm clothes and were about to set off on the long drive when Purohit tapped David on the shoulder.

'Soldier, drop us off at our place please.'

Everyone started protesting at once, but Purohit raised a hand to silence them.

'Look, you have a more important mission than dragging along a couple of old men. Get that boy to someone who can figure out why he's immune and use it to help all of us.'

'Your *not* coming along will make us weaker!' Mayukh said.

Purohit smiled.

'No, we would be a liability. Lamba's got asthma and I have a busted leg from an old war wound. We would just slow you down, especially in the hills. No, my friends, this is where the Bartender takes his last stand. Go on now; Lamba and I need to get ready before sunset. You see, we old fogeys will do some hunting tonight.'

Mayukh was about to protest again, but David stopped him. 'He's right,' he whispered.

Mayukh saw that, despite his words, the American soldier looked almost choked with emotion. As they dropped the two old men, David got out, stood at attention and saluted both of them.

'Captain David Bremsak requesting orders to proceed on mission, sir.'

Purohit saluted back, smiling broadly, his eyes glinting with a hint of tears.

'Happy hunting, Captain.'

David drove for the first hour or so, and then Mayukh relieved him at the wheel. Swati was in the front seat next to him, with Abhi on her lap. The little boy kept up an incessant chatter that had everyone distracted, something they were all thankful for. Otherwise, they would have perhaps dwelt more on the desolate landscape they passed.

The national highway they were on was usually a death trap at night, with its heavy trucks driven by overworked and often drunk drivers. Now it was eerily empty. A few trucks lay abandoned by the roadside, but there were no moving vehicles or people in sight. Abhi was looking out the window and giving a running commentary on what he saw.

'I saw a big red truck.'

'There's a giant blue truck which is broken.'

Mayukh smiled at Abhi's exuberance, trying to suppress the anxiety he felt. He caught himself looking at Swati now and then, and though her eyes showed fatigue and stress, she smiled back. He wondered about the convoluted ways in which fate worked. He had lost everything he had taken to be his own, only to find someone like her in the midst of all this chaos. The feelings he had for her, and the trust Abhi had placed in him, both made him feel incredibly protective, and also woefully under-qualified for the task of protecting them. He glanced back at David whose face was an inscrutable mask as he stared out the window.

David was consumed with the logistics of the task they were faced with. As much as he would have liked to believe otherwise, he knew their chances were slim. He was down to two clips for his M4, and while he had a lot of ammunition for his handgun, that was of little use at long range. Mayukh was down to ten rounds, and while he had proven to be a brave young man, he was no trained soldier. Add to that the motley crew an old woman, a young girl and a toddler, and he figured their chances of making it through a hostile landscape teeming with psychotic zombies didn't look very good.

That, of course, didn't mean he wouldn't do his best to get himself and everyone else out alive. He had Rose to get back to, and if what they all said about the kid was indeed true, then perhaps there was something worth fighting for after all.

Mayukh thought that Hina was handling the stress the best, fussing over them, handing out regular instalments of cookies and snacks, and telling them they needed to keep their energy and spirits up. Swati, too, seemed calm and composed.

Hina would never have admitted it, but her enthusiasm

came from an unlikely source. She had been used to solitude for years, with nothing and nobody to care for but herself. Somewhere, she had secretly longed to fuss over her grandchildren, to pester her children to eat well, to say good night to someone before she went to sleep. Now, for better or worse, she had people to take care of. She so wanted to believe that getting Abhi to safety would indeed lift the darkness that had enveloped the world. Also, the romantic in her wanted to make sure that Mayukh and Swati got a chance to live a normal life together, a life where they would not have to fight to survive from one day to another.

Their journey thus continued, each of them consumed with their own hopes and worries, except Abhi, who was happy to simply look at the trucks he saw by the roadside and gobble down the cookies that Hina passed to him on demand.

They had driven for just over three hours and it was past four in the evening. David suggested they start planning on where to spend the night. The map he had open on his lap gave him an obvious answer.

Karnal.

It was a small town on the way to Manali, the popular tourist hill station that was the gateway to the mountainous passes that led to Ladakh. None of them had been there before, but it was a safe bet that they would find an abandoned home where they could seek refuge for the night.

They drove past a few old houses when they spotted something totally unexpected. A few hundred metres away, on the roadside, a bright neon sign lit up the otherwise barren and darkening landscape. The sign read 'Zilmil Restaurant. Five-star food, one-star prices'.

Mayukh looked at David, who shrugged, as if to say 'why not'.

Mayukh brought the SUV to a halt in the narrow driveway outside the small, nondescript shack. David asked for the others to stay in the vehicle and stepped out, his rifle at the ready. He approached the building cautiously, sweeping the area in front of him. He flattened himself against the wall and peered in through the open window. Satisfied, he signalled to the others to join him.

As they came closer, he whispered to Hina and Swati to stay a few steps behind with Abhi and asked Mayukh to cover him. He kicked open the door, and dived in, rolling on the floor and coming up in a crouch, his weapon at his shoulder. Mayukh was at the door, his pistol in front of him, hoping that he wouldn't have to use it.

The little roadside eatery with five-star pretensions had a few cheap plastic tables and chairs, and a kitchen area in a corner blocked by a large counter. There was a slight humming noise, probably coming from the generator that was powering the neon sign outside.

Mayukh thought he heard something, and he looked at David to confirm that he wasn't just imagining it. David nodded to indicate that he too had heard it. Mayukh heard it again, and he would have found it almost funny had they all not been so much on edge.

It was the sound of someone hiccupping.

David pointed behind the counter. Mayukh nodded, moving slowly behind David as he approached the counter.

David leaned over, his gun at the ready, and then lowered it, yanking out with one hand the person who had been hiding there.

The man was scrawny to the point of looking like a famine victim, and wore torn shorts and a vest that must have once been white, but was now coated a dirty brown. His hair was matted, and his face looked like he had been smeared with soot. Despite all that, his eyes shone brightly and he was smiling broadly, revealing white teeth.

'Welcome to Zilmil Restaurant. We offer five-star food at one-star prices.'

He hiccupped again, and Abhi giggled.

The man's eyes lit up as he saw Abhi; he laughed aloud in delight, and moved towards the little boy.

'Hello, little one. Do you want some ice cream?'

Abhi was about to go over to him, but Swati held his hand tightly. David tensed, half bringing up his rifle.

As if oblivious to the fact that he was facing two armed men, the man suddenly pirouetted, held out his hand to Mayukh and said, 'I have totally forgotten my manners. My name is Freddy, and welcome to my humble little restaurant.'

Then he skipped over to where Hina stood.

'Madam, would you like some coffee?'

Hina nodded, just wanting the strange man to shut up or go away.

Freddy ran over to the counter, pulled a cup out from behind it, and, handing the empty cup over to Hina, said, 'Be careful, it's very hot.'

Abhi was enjoying the man's antics, and he piped up, 'Blow into it to cool it!'

Freddy clapped his hands in delight. 'Smart boy!'

David had now lowered his weapon and walked up to Mayukh. 'The poor man has lost his mind.'

Freddy turned to David and said in immaculate English, 'No, no! I have not lost my mind, sir. I assure you that I am fully in control of my faculties. Here, have some tea.'

He picked up another empty cup and handed it to David, and then disappeared into the back of the restaurant, mumbling something about finding some food for his guests.

Swati and Abhi moved closer to Mayukh and he reached out for her hand.

Hina said softly, 'Poor, poor man. I wonder what he must have gone through for him to go over the edge like this.'

They heard Freddy call out to them to join him in the back. They moved there cautiously, and saw that he was dragging a carpet, thereby revealing, to their astonishment, a trapdoor. Freddy opened it with considerable effort and looked at them.

'The sun is about to go down. Now they will come out to play hide-and-seek. Will you play with me?'

David motioned for the others to stay put, and climbed down the ladder he found under the trapdoor. A few seconds later, he called for the others to join him.

They found a small room that had been created to store supplies, and it was currently stocked with bags of rice, sugar, biscuits and other staples, but there was enough room for all of them to sit down. Freddy was the last to climb down, and they saw him adjust the carpet before he closed the door. He scrambled down the ladder and flipped a switch on the wall, and a single bulb lit up the darkness.

Freddy sat down and opened a pack of biscuits and passed them around. Abhi grabbed two of them and wolfed them down with gusto.

David asked Freddy what he had been through, but all he got in response was a rambling description of his secret tandoori chicken recipe that was the talk of Karnal.

Suddenly Freddy put his fingers on his lips.

'Now we all need to be good boys and girls and we need to sleep tight. If we make any noise, they will come. Good night.'

He turned off the bulb, curled up in a corner and closed his eyes.

They all looked at each other and Mayukh saw a hint of amusement creep into Swati's eyes, replaced immediately by a look of guilt.

'What happened?'

She put her head against his shoulder.

'I was about to say something about him being crazy, but he probably saved our lives tonight.'

They were all on edge, but soon fatigue got the better of them, and one by one, they fell into an uneasy sleep.

Mayukh had Swati with her head resting on his left shoulder and Abhi curled up on his lap. He would never have imagined being in such a situation just days ago, but before he drifted off to sleep, he thought that he had never been so happy.

Shuffling noises directly overhead their hiding place awakened him, and then he heard the screeching howls of the Biters. He had heard it many times now, but it still sent a shiver down his spine. He looked around and in the darkness could make out the others stirring. They all sat huddled together, praying that the Biters would not find them and would move on.

The Biters seemed to be trashing Freddy's modest restaurant, judging by the crashing and ripping noises they heard.

David whispered to Mayukh, 'I screwed up. We left our car outside. If these Biters *are* getting smarter, they know we must be around and are looking for us.'

The reminder that the creatures were gradually becoming sentient, and yet were as bloodthirsty as before, struck fear in all of them. David sat with his rifle pointed at the hatch, hoping that he would not have to use it.

Finally, after what seemed an eternity, the Biters left. The hidden group was covered in sweat despite the winter chill, and nearly everyone jumped when Freddy turned on the bulb. Despite all that had happened, he was smiling. He clapped his hands together.

'We won our game of hide-and-seek again. Now we can go out and play. Welcome to Zilmil Restaurant. Five-star food at one-star prices!'

They emerged one by one, relieved to see that it was daytime while taking in the extent to which the restaurant had been damaged. The Biters had taken it apart piece by piece, smashing furniture and crockery, leaving it looking as if a tornado had spun through it. The devastation did not seem to dampen Freddy's enthusiasm; he picked up a half-smashed cup and offered Abhi tea. The boy squealed with laughter and soon they were playing a game of hide-and-seek. That gave the adults some time to plan. David was about to suggest they leave immediately, when he looked out the window.

'Oh, shit!'

They ran out to see the windows of their SUV smashed open and scratches and dents crisscrossing its sides. Mayukh's heart sank as he wondered what they would do if the vehicle didn't start.

David ran to it and tried the ignition. To everyone's relief, the engine fired up.

Swati sighed with relief. 'Thankfully they aren't that smart.' She added, in a lower tone. 'Yet.'

They managed to pry Abhi from Freddy, who asked them to leave Abhi with him as a playmate and seemed genuinely hurt when they told him Abhi was going with them. Hina looked pleadingly towards David and asked if they could take Freddy with them. David instantly refused.

As much as Mayukh felt sorry for the man, he realised that with the long journey that lay ahead of them, he would be a liability. As they were about to drive away, Freddy ran up to the window where Mayukh was sitting.

'They say there is an ashram in Manali where the Biters don't go. If you get hungry, don't go there but come back to Zilmil Restaurant. Remember, five-star food at one-star prices.'

Mayukh smiled and waved goodbye, but then something seemed to occur to Freddy and he gripped Mayukh's arm, speaking with a seriousness that Mayukh had not heard in his voice before.

'Be careful. The Biters are not the only ones to hide from. There are those who come in the day.'

Eight

According to the guidebook, it was a good eight- to ten-hour drive from Karnal to Manali, the last gateway to the mountain passes that would lead to Ladakh. With its large number of guesthouses, they had hoped to find some refuge in Manali for the night before they set out again the next morning.

The problem, David thought, as he tried to focus on the road ahead, was that there was no way they were going to get anywhere close to Manali by sunset. With the front windshield smashed, they could not drive very fast. He quickly conferred with the others, and they agreed that if it looked like they were not going to get to Manali by sunset, then they would stop at the town of Mandi.

They had been driving for a couple of hours with Abhi dozing on Hina's lap. Mayukh was in the front passenger seat, and he felt behind him for Swati's hand, holding it as the trip continued.

'Do you lovebirds want to move to the backseat?'

Swati blushed at Hina's comment, but Mayukh noted with a smile that she did not let go of his hand. It was funny how things were so different because of the situation. Those of his friends who had girlfriends spent weeks courting them with emails and texts and phone calls before they went on that first date. Their first 'date' had involved being chased around by undead creatures called Biters!

Abhi woke up and, looking out the back windshield, asked sleepily, 'Is it cloudy today?'

Swati tousled her baby brother's hair.

'No, Abhi, it's actually quite sunny, but see we have no windows, so it feels windy.'

Still, Abhi was insistent.

'No, look *there*! It's very cloudy there.'

Mayukh had turned around to look at Abhi, and now his gaze followed Abhi's pointing finger. In the distance, he could see a rolling cloud of dust being raised on the approaches leading to the highway.

'What is that?' Hina asked David.

David glanced in the rear-view mirror and then turned around for a better look. His face tightened as he responded.

'At least two or three vehicles, coming at high speed.'

In a few more seconds, they could see them—three jeeps, with at least four men in each vehicle. Swati murmured hopefully, 'Maybe they're also trying to get to safety, like us.'

Just then, one of the men in the leading jeep took out a pistol and fired three shots. Moving at high speed, the shots came nowhere near their vehicle, but it confirmed that the three jeeps bearing down on them were hardly coming to offer assistance.

'Get down and stay down! There's no way we can outrun them.'

Those in the backseat needed no more encouragement from David as Hina and Swati both hit the deck, pulling Abhi with them. The boy asked why they were hiding in the daytime, but nobody had the time to answer him.

David motioned for Mayukh to take the wheel, and he slid

to the other side while trying to keep the SUV straight. They would have looked ludicrous in any other circumstance, with David half sitting on Mayukh's lap and leaning out the window. But there was nothing funny about what he had in mind. He asked Mayukh for his rifle and then took aim at the jeep in the middle.

Two more of their pursuers were firing their handguns, and a few shots were pinged off the SUV. David fired a carefully aimed three-round burst and the windshield on the jeep shattered as the shots hit home, killing the driver instantly. The jeep careened over to the side of the road and toppled over, and the men standing in the back were thrown onto the road by the impact.

The other two jeeps spread out and continued the chase, steadily gaining on the SUV.

'Mayukh, they're spreading out. I can't get them both.'

Mayukh was wondering what to do when Swati shouted, 'Give me your gun!'

She leaned out the window with the gun, and fired at one of the pursuing jeeps till the clip ran empty. She didn't hit anything or anyone, but the surprise of being met with such firepower caused the jeep to slow down and veer to the left, where it entered David's field of fire.

By now David had unloaded a dozen rounds into the other jeep, several hitting the driver and sending the jeep rolling end on end till it landed in a heap by the side of the road. The third jeep, having moved from Swati's side, was now a mere twenty metres away and three men in it were firing away with handguns. Mayukh heard David gasp in pain as he fell back into the SUV, accidentally colliding with Mayukh and causing him to lose control. He heard a whooshing noise as the vehicle buckled and started swerving to the right, as he struggled to control it.

'Bastards shot out one of our tyres,' David exclaimed through clenched teeth as he felt his wound, his hand coming back covered with blood.

'Are you okay? That looks pretty bad,' Hina said.

David nodded. 'Just a flesh wound,' he said, and added sombrely, 'We have to stand and fight now. We don't have a choice.'

As the SUV slowly rolled to a halt by the roadside, David did something unexpected. He opened the door and rolled outside onto the road. The jeep's occupants saw him and began firing at him as he ran to the other side of the road, diving to take cover behind a road sign.

Mayukh took his gun from Swati, loaded his last clip and stood outside the vehicle, aiming at the jeep that was now bearing down on David.

He had fired at one of the goons attacking Swati, and then at the Biters outside Purohit's apartment. But this was different. It was the first time he was shooting to kill a human being. David was not returning fire; he was either out of ammunition or more badly wounded than he had admitted. Either way, Mayukh knew it all came down to him.

He steadied his hands, spreading his legs slightly and bending at the knee to get the best balance. He remembered what his father had once taught him. Always shoot between heartbeats. He aimed just ahead of the driver and pulled the trigger twice in quick succession.

The first bullet hit the man in the hip and the second,

raised by the slight recoil of the gun, hit him in the chest. The jeep swerved to the side as the driver fell out. He did not get up again.

Mayukh had no time to contemplate what he had done. The three remaining men jumped from the jeep, guns in hand, and turned towards him. A bullet pinged off the SUV, inches from his face, as he knelt down and fired at the shooter. Three shots in rapid succession, two of which struck home. The man went down hard against the jeep, bounced to the ground and stayed down.

Mayukh felt a stinging pain sear through his leg and he fell. Another man had fired at him, and the bullet had grazed his hip.

That was when David exploded into action. He raced out from behind cover, his handgun raised, firing as he ran. He emptied the clip into the man nearest to him, who was struck by round after round, pirouetting like a puppet on a string before he fell. David discarded the gun, took his combat knife in hand and jumped on the man who had just shot Mayukh.

The man turned to face him and tried to raise his gun, but he never stood a chance. He may have won numerous drunken brawls, but facing a Navy SEAL out to kill him, he lasted no more than three seconds.

The others were outside the car. Abhi ran to Mayukh, hugging his knee and crying.

Swati hugged him close as he tried to get up. 'Oh god, I thought you were ...'

There was no need to say anything more. Mayukh held her close, as David walked over. His right shoulder was covered in blood.

'Ah shucks, I wish someone would fuss over me as well. I'm bleeding too, you know.'

Hina laughed. 'All you get is a sixty-five-year-old crone.'

She took out the first-aid pack from the car and tended to his wound.

David and Mayukh had both suffered superficial wounds that were soon bandaged. They continued to sit by the highway for some minutes, revelling in the close escape they'd had.

Mayukh looked at Swati, who was feeding Abhi some cookies. 'You were really brave back there.'

Swati said something about not even hitting anything, but David nodded in agreement.

'He's right, Swati. You probably saved us.'

None of them had yet asked the question that was on everyone's mind. How would they ever get to Manali or to anywhere safe before sunset? The SUV's spare tyre had been slashed by the Biters. Two of the jeeps that had pursued them were wrecks, and the third was leaking fuel from two bullet holes. It was already two in the afternoon, and nobody had any bright ideas. They were also running short on ammunition: David was out of ammunition for his rifle, and was on his last clip for his handgun, and Mayukh had only four rounds left.

David inspected the weapons of their attackers to see if there was anything useful. But they were all crude country-made pistols.

Hina rested her head against the SUV's side, her eyes closed. Her heart was still hammering, and as she began to think of the dangers they had all faced and the stakes each of them had in the struggle to get to Ladakh, she thought about how little she mattered. David was their unspoken leader due to his military experience; Swati and Mayukh had each other and Abhi to live and fight for; and the little boy was the key to this whole expedition, the one spark of hope that kept them all going. But what was she doing in all this? She couldn't fight, she had no useful skills to offer, and nobody who would lament her passing.

Mayukh shouted, 'Shit, not again!'

All of them looked up: a cloud of smoke was approaching them on the highway.

Hina, Swati and Abhi crouched inside the SUV, while David took cover behind one open door, and Mayukh, the other. They had just over a dozen rounds between them, but they were hoping to catch whoever it was in their crossfire.

As the black van came closer, David aimed at the driver, and was about to fire, when the van stopped and a single man stepped out, his hands in the air, and began walking towards them.

As he came closer, they saw that he was Caucasian, totally bald and wearing jeans and a plain white shirt. His hands were raised, and as he came within a few feet, he said loudly, with a thick accent, 'I am here to help.'

Mayukh got up and started to move towards the man, but David motioned for him to wait, his gun still pointing at the stranger.

'That's close enough. Who are you?'

The man looked at David and smiled.

'My name is Walter. I am alone and unarmed.'

The way he said his name, it sounded like *Valter*.

Hina and Swati emerged from the vehicle, and the man waved to them. He seemed friendly enough, but after all they had been through, David was not about to take any chances.

'Walter, what are you doing out here all alone?'

The man dropped his hands, causing David to tense, but then he laughed.

'Come on, you have two armed young men covering me. I am fifty and have no weapons on me. Let me come closer and I can tell you more. By all means, keep your guns on me, if that makes you feel better, but don't make me shout through this conversation.'

David nodded and the man approached them. Up close, they could see that the man was very fit: there was not an ounce of spare fat on his body, and his arms were sinewy and muscled. His face, however, was creased and wrinkled with age. He smiled again as he came up to them.

'I do this route twice every day, looking for people like you.'

'What do you mean?' David asked.

The man pointed to the overturned jeeps and carnage around them. 'There are many like them, preying on the weak and desperate. And then, there are the Biters. It appears that safety is a precious commodity nowadays. Thankfully, we have safety to offer. And we try and help as many people there as we can.'

'Who is we?' Mayukh asked.

The man's expression indicated that he would have thought

that everyone knew about the sanctuary he was referring to. 'The Sammasati Ashram in Kullu, of course.'

Mayukh remembered the ashram Freddy of the one-star price had referred to. David must have remembered as well, for he visibly relaxed, lowering his gun, though he did not put it back in its holster. Walter took this as a good sign, and came closer, still smiling and nodding politely to Hina and Swati.

Abhi bounded out of the SUV and looked at the stranger in their midst. He giggled and said, 'You have no hair.'

Everyone tried their best to suppress their laughter as Walter knelt in front of Abhi.

'No, my dear, I have not had hair for many years now. But I do have a toy train set back at the ashram. You could play with that, if you like. Would you like that?'

Abhi's eyes lit up and he looked at Swati, as if seeking permission. David asked Walter how they had set up the ashram, and how many people were there. Walter looked at his watch.

'My friend, it's almost three in the afternoon. Even if I drive as fast as I dare to with all the abandoned trucks and cars on the highway up ahead, we will barely get there by sunset. Come with me, and I can tell you everything you want on the way. But you have to trust me at least that much.'

Asking Walter for a minute to discuss it, the adults huddled together a few paces away.

Mayukh spoke first, keeping an eye on Abhi, who was now happily chatting with the stranger. 'We don't have much of a choice, do we? We're stranded here, we're almost out of ammunition and in about three hours, if those Biters are indeed looking for us, then we have almost zero chances of getting through the night.'

David looked at Hina and Swati, as if seeking their agreement. They both nodded and Hina added with a whisper.

'I don't like when I am forced to do something because there's no other option available, but in this case, we have to go with him.'

Each of them looked at the little boy, and was reminded of what the stakes really were. Whatever their misgivings about joining this stranger, they knew only too well that Abhi had to be protected, and if there was even a remote possibility that the Biters were indeed trying to target him, then they could not take any chances.

They walked back to Walter, and David finally held out his hand and introduced himself. Walter shook it with a broad grin and then asked them to get their stuff and join him in his van.

A few minutes later, they set off with Walter at the wheel.

Looking at Swati's anxious face, Mayukh knew she was thinking the same thing they all were.

Had they made the right decision in joining this stranger?

The first thing David noticed when he sat down in the front passenger seat was the shotgun lying on the floor. That wasn't much of a surprise—anyone expecting to be driving alone in these times would reasonably be expected to have some means of defending himself. The second thing he noticed did take him by surprise. Walter had a small radio transmitter set, also on the floor, and it seemed to be connected by wires to the battery for power. When he turned on the ignition, it flared to life.

'Bald Eagle, where are you? You don't have much more time.'

Abhi screamed from the backseat.

'Yes, Uncle is bald, bald, bald!'

Mayukh and Swati tried not to laugh, while Hina, red with embarrassment, asked Abhi to be quiet, but the boy continued his chant, but at a slightly lower volume.

Walter tut-tutted and picked up the attached microphone to respond over the radio.

'Guruji, I am on my way. I have picked up some friends. Over.'

David waited for a few minutes before bringing up the subject.

'You guys seem very organised.'

Walter responded without taking his eyes off the road.

'We have to be. There are three hundred people at the ashram now, and we need to be organised to both take care of their needs and also find and help others like you.'

'Three hundred! How did so many ...'

Hina left her question unfinished but Walter responded, looking at her in the mirror.

'Take me for example. An Austrian businessman on holiday in Manali. Then all hell breaks loose. Where could I go? The cops had died, run away or become Biters. I stumbled upon the ashram where Guruji was, and together with some others, under his guidance, we started off. As word spread, more and more people sought us out.'

'You mentioned Guruji again. Who is he?'

'He's the one holding it all together. I gather he was well known in India. His name is Swami Vinesh.'

Despite himself, Mayukh sniggered and he turned to see that Swati was rolling her eyes. Hina, unlike the young people, managed to just nod in response. David, noticing their responses, turned and asked Mayukh who Swami Vinesh was.

'He's a godman, or so he claims. Started off teaching yoga, and then became a guru to politicians and movie stars. He has his own TV channel now, and a private jet. And he nominated himself for the Nobel Peace Prize.'

'Are you pulling my leg?'

Hina piped in. 'I think Mayukh is being quite diplomatic. He was caught in a sex scandal last year when he was taped asking a devotee for sexual favours, which he said would get her nirvana. Nice to know we're going to be his guests.'

David, now not so sure they had made the right choice after all, looked towards Walter, who shrugged his shoulders.

'Look, I know nothing about his past or if what they say about him is true or not. All I know is that he is selflessly helping hundreds of people survive this hell. That makes him a good guy in my book.'

They drove the rest of the way in silence, each of them wondering what lay ahead. After about an hour more, as the sunlight beginning to fade, they saw a group of huts ahead. As they passed the shelters, David's experienced eyes picked up what the others had not noticed.

'Ambush points with gunmen inside.'

If Walter heard it, he did not say anything but kept driving till they reached a complex surrounded by a wooden fence that was at least twelve feet high. They saw that the fence was ringed with torches that were in the process of being lit, and by the time they reached the massive wooden gate, the complex was lit up like a giant birthday cake.

As they came closer, the gate swung open and they entered the complex.

Mayukh's first impression was that it resembled a holiday resort more than an ashram, with villas lining the street that cut through the complex and trees bursting with apples and flowers. He could see a handful of people around, but what immediately got his attention was the group of armed men who approached the van as it stopped. There were three men, all Caucasian and each carrying a shotgun, with a pistol tucked into his belt.

Seeing them approach, David's hand went to his handgun, but Walter spoke in a reassuring voice.

'Relax. They are friends. They help look after security here, that's all.'

As they got down from the van, they huddled as a group and Walter exchanged some words with the three men. One of them, an overweight man with an immense gut, approached them, speaking in a heavy Slavic accent.

'Ve vill need to take your gunz.'

It took David a second to process what the man meant, but when he understood he smiled, sizing up his opponent. The man was more than six feet tall, and had muscular arms and a thick neck, but the muscle he must have built during his youth had dissipated into the fat that lined his waist. He carried his shotgun like an amateur, with his hand gripping it in the middle like a baseball bat.

David, his senses honed by countless hours of training and combat, knew in a split second that he could fell him with his gun or knife before the man ever got his gun into firing position. But a second later, he forced himself to calm down. There were other armed men around, and even if he might have been tempted to take his chances if he were alone, there was no scope for heroics with the others depending on him, especially Abhi. But there was no way he was going to give up their only means of defending themselves.

He turned to Walter, who seemed to be watching expectantly, as if waiting to see how David would react.

'Walter, please tell your friends that I take my orders only from my superiors in the US military, and till someone in my chain of command tells me to stand down, I am on active combat duty.'

The fat man in front of him did not seem to be very pleased, but Walter stuck out his hand, showing a thumbs-up sign.

'Of course, Captain. My friends have not dealt with any soldiers yet. They mean no disrespect, but they are just trying to ensure everyone here remains secure.'

They were ushered to a villa to the left that had a hand-lettered sign hanging on the front saying 'Administrative Office'. The interior looked like a fully functional office, with shelves lined with files and desks where people seemed hard at work. Two desks were occupied by radio operators sitting in front of hand-cranked radio sets.

As they walked in, Walter whispered, 'You won't believe

the paperwork it takes to feed and keep three hundred souls alive and safe. Inventories of supplies, records of fights or disagreements, even rumours of illicit romances.'

He smiled, but David was impressed. Whoever this Swami Vinesh was, and whatever his history had been, it was clear that he was running a very tight ship here. They approached a desk where a thin man wearing glasses was sitting, scribbling something into a thick file.

He looked up at the newcomers and without any niceties said in a slightly nasal voice, 'I am P.C. Sharma, the administrator here. Please tell us your name, age, occupation and where you are coming from.'

Mayukh and Swati went first and when David introduced himself, Sharma raised his eyebrows a bit, perhaps wondering what he was doing in India. He asked Swati for Abhi's name, but the boy stepped forward and gave it himself.

'Abhimanyu Talwar.'

The man smiled and said, 'You are a cute boy. Do you want a chocolate?'

Abhi scowled. 'My mama told me never to take chocolates from strangers.'

Suitably chastened, Sharma called Hina over. She stood in front of the table and said her name. Sharma looked up, and then at Walter, who just shrugged his shoulders. He then asked Hina to repeat her name.

'Hina Rahman. Is there a problem?'

Sharma seemed to get into a state of considerable agitation and then he called out loudly for someone.

'Vineet, come here quickly!'

A short, chubby man walked over and Sharma whispered something to him. He too looked at Hina, his eyes hardening. Hina had taken a step back, not sure what the problem was, but not liking what she saw.

Mayukh had never really liked the look of Walter's friends at the gate, and now Sharma's behaviour was giving him the creeps. His gun was tucked into his belt and he put his hand on his waist, so that if there was any trouble, he would be able to react quickly. The problem was that it was now dark outside, and he had no idea where they could go if they were not welcome here.

Finally, Sharma approached David, assuming he was leading the group, and pulled him aside. Mayukh also went over, eager to learn what the problem was.

'The problem is that I am not sure we should let her type in here.'

David was bewildered at the man's statement.

'What on earth do you mean? Do you mean her age?'

Sharma shook his head and said, as if he were explaining something to a small child, 'No, no. She is one of *them*.'

When David still didn't seem to get it, he blurted out, perhaps louder than he would have liked, 'She is Muslim! She cannot stay here. Don't you get it? All those Biters started among jihadis in Afghanistan; they wear those damned turbans and keep screaming about jihad!'

Hina gasped and Mayukh sensed her moving closer to Swati, as if seeking safety. David was still processing what the man had said, but being much closer to the religious fanaticism and hate that gripped many in India, Mayukh exploded with rage, 'You frigging moron! The world has gone to hell and you're worried about your petty religious hatred. She is one of us and she stays.'

His hand was curled into a fist, and he didn't doubt that if Sharma said one word more, he would hit him. Walter had stepped out of the villa, but his overweight friend who had accosted them at the gate stepped towards Mayukh, shotgun in his left hand.

'You vill listen to the man!' he said, and extending his right hand, he grabbed at Mayukh.

As he did so, David stepped in between them. The man must have outweighed David by a handsome margin and was a good three to four inches taller than him, but then he didn't have an iota of the training in unarmed combat David had.

David caught his right wrist in one hand and then pirouetted on his heel, twisting the man's arm, bringing him kneeling to the ground, his arm bent behind him. The man's face contorted in pain, and the shotgun fell from his hand.

'Down, boy. Don't get too excited here. If you move, I'll break your arm and then snap the little twerp's neck there.'

He had said it in an even voice, but Sharma shrank back in fear.

David knew they had crossed a line. The problem was that, even if they managed to get out, with it being dark outside, he had no idea how he could keep them safe.

NINE

Mayukh suddenly heard Walter, his voice still even and calm despite the tension in the room.

'Captain Bremsak, please let my friend Mikhail go. He was just doing his job. I assure you this is nothing but a misunderstanding.'

David just snorted in disdain and reached for his gun so that Walter would not catch him by surprise.

Mayukh stepped towards Walter. 'You brought us here claiming that you would provide us with safety. Now your friend here refuses to take one of us because of her religion. What kind of a place do you run here?'

Just then, a man dressed in saffron robes walked in. Mayukh recognised him immediately: he had seen those piercing blue eyes, flowing hair and lean features on TV many times. He spoke in a soothing voice.

'Violence and anger only beget more anger. Walter, Sharma, Mikhail, you have not treated our guests well. Please, everyone, calm down. This is a place of peace, a shared sanctuary for all of us in these troubled times, and rest assured, each and every one of you is welcome here.'

He then walked up to Hina and bowed his head slightly.

'My apologies for my colleague's words. We are all children of God, even if we try and reach him in different ways. It's just that with all the unfortunate events of the last few days, everyone is stressed—and many are giving in to their worst fears and prejudices. Please friends, calm down and join us here.'

David relaxed a bit and asked him who he was.

The man smiled at him. 'I am your humble host for the evening. My name is Swami Vinesh.'

The godman told them that he would meet with them personally in a few minutes, but first they had an evening ritual where everybody at the ashram met for dinner, and caught up with what had happened in the day, updating each other on what was going on in the outside world.

Mikhail still looked at them with scarcely contained fury, but the others seemed to have taken Swami Vinesh's cue and welcomed the new arrivals.

They were escorted to their villas: Hina, Swati and Abhi would share one, and David and Mayukh were in the adjoining one. The first thing Mayukh noticed was that they had running hot water.

P.C. Sharma, who had accompanied them to the villa, smiled. 'We have a diesel-powered generator, and the ashram's been pumping its own fresh water for years, but we do have limited fuel stocks, so we run the hot water only for an hour a day. Guess you're lucky you arrived when it was on.'

Mayukh took the longest bath he'd ever had, scrubbing himself clean, trying to wash off not only the accumulated sweat, dust and filth of the last few days, but also hoping that he could somehow erase the terrible memories of what he had seen and gone through. When he came out of the bathroom, he found loose-fitting saffron pyjamas and t-shirts on his bed. They made him look like a hippie, but he was grateful for the clean clothes.

When David was done with his shower, they met up with the others, and followed Sharma to a courtyard. There were several dozen people already there, and without consciously realising it, Mayukh and the others moved closer together. Mayukh was holding Swati's hand with his right and Abhi's with his left. Hina was barely a step behind, and David, ever their sentinel, walked one step ahead of them, scanning the group. In a short few days, they had come to trust and depend on each other to a degree that they would never have believed possible when they had first been thrown together.

David felt a bit out of place carrying his handgun tucked into his belt, since nobody else seemed to be armed, but he didn't want to take any chances, especially after the incident in the office. There was no sign of Walter, Mikhail or the other armed men they had met at the gate, and when David asked Sharma where they were, he said they were standing guard at the walls.

'There are so many of them!' Swati whispered to Mayukh, and he could but nod in agreement. Looking at the people milling around the courtyard, he saw entire families, foreign tourists, even a couple with a little dog. It felt like an eternity since he had last encountered such a large crowd of people, not counting Biters out to rip his throat out, of course. Many of those around turned to stare at the newcomers, but Mayukh saw no hostility, just vacant glances, and even a few wan smiles. As he walked through the crowd, most of them seemed to be totally engrossed in what Swami Vinesh was saying, as if hypnotised by him.

The swami was standing on a slightly raised platform facing the crowd.

'We—me, you, all of us—are like a candle burning in the darkness. A symbol that all hope is not lost. A sign that no matter the horrors that have threatened to take over our world, we can survive if we stick together. Is that not what religion is all about? Binding people together? I thank you all for helping maintain this oasis that we have created, and pray that God gives us all the strength and faith to persevere.'

'Damn, he has them eating out of the palm of his hand.'

Mayukh smiled at David's comment, but seeing the swami in person for the first time, he'd realised why he had such a following. Whatever else he may be, he certainly had tons of charisma.

Abhi suddenly broke away from Mayukh's grasp and ran forward.

'Abhi!'

Mayukh got up to run after the boy, who was making a beeline for the swami. The swami faltered in his speech, and then smiled broadly and held out his arms to embrace the boy. But Abhi ran right past him and behind the platform. The swami got up with an embarrassed look on his face, and some people in the crowd tittered.

Mayukh scampered past the platform to see Abhi pick up a toy car. He looked at Mayukh, his face beaming.

'I found McQueen!'

Mayukh wondered whose car it was and tried to take it away from Abhi.

'Abhi, that's not your car. Remember, we left it in the bookstore? This just looks like your car.'

But Abhi was adamant and tears started streaming down his face.

'No! This is my McQueen.'

The swami had now come up beside Mayukh, who looked at him apologetically.

The swami smiled. 'Please, you have nothing to feel sorry for. A child's innocence is one of the most beautiful things God has blessed us with. Little one, do you want this car?'

Abhi nodded vigorously, and when the swami told him he could have it, he shouted in delight and ran back to where Swati was and began playing with it, oblivious to the disruption he had caused.

A few minutes later, the swami invited the newcomers to his villa, which to their surprise had been stripped of all the luxurious furnishings which their villas contained, and instead had a simple mattress on the floor and a small writing table.

'For some, simple living is a cliché; for me it is the best way to realise God.'

David whispered to Mayukh, 'Is this guy for real? Call me cynical, but whenever anyone is so holier-than-thou, my bullshit alarm goes off.'

Mayukh tried not to laugh as Swami Vinesh asked them to sit on the floor near him. Swati had been worried that it was close to Abhi's bedtime, but the boy was so busy playing with the car, that he barely noticed anything or anyone. David and Mayukh didn't know what the Swami wanted of them, and were a bit surprised when Hina took the lead in the discussion.

'Swami Vinesh, what happened here?'

The swami reached for a glass of water next to his mattress and replied, 'I was teaching meditation here to about a hundred of my disciples when the problems began. When we began to understand the full extent of the trouble after the second night, we barricaded ourselves in. As you have seen, the walls and gate are quite formidable.'

Hina didn't seem satisfied.

'But not formidable enough to keep those fiends out. David has seen them tear apart armed and trained troops, and we have all seen the havoc they unleashed in the cities. How do you keep them out, and where do Walter and his friends fit in?'

Mayukh thought he saw a flicker of irritation cross the Swami's face, but then it was quickly replaced by his usual expression of beatific calm.

'Walter can explain more about our defences. I am hardly a man of action. My biggest responsibility is to keep those in here—my original devotees and the dozens who came in from neighbouring villages and hotels—safe as long as I can.'

David had been studying the swami, and asked the question that was on his mind. 'Excuse me, Swami Vinesh, I'll ask Walter about your defences, but how long can you hold up in here? You seem pretty well organised, but sooner or later, food and fuel will run out.'

Mayukh once again got the impression that the swami was not accustomed to—and not particularly happy with—being asked so many questions.

'Captain, every day we go to neighbouring towns and villages to stock up. Sharma, my assistant, tells me that we should be good for at least a couple of months, provided we don't take in any more such as you.'

David smiled. So the swami had a bite after all. However, whatever they felt about the man, the reality was that if Walter had not picked them up, they'd have been on their own outside, in the dark, at this very moment.

'Now, it's my turn to ask some questions. Where were you headed?'

Mayukh responded. 'You have radios here. You must have heard the Ladakh announcement. Why don't you go there? You're not that far. That's where we are going, and with Abhi—'

Before he could complete the sentence, Swati gripped his hand so hard her nails dug into his skin.

'Yes, yes. Ladakh. We have talked about it, but we are waiting for more than just some anonymous announcements. In here, we are safe for now. Out there, we are a largely defenceless group of civilians. What if this Ladakh sanctuary, if it ever existed, has fallen?'

Before they returned to their respective villas, they paused to confer in low voices.

Hina was very clear on what she wanted.

'We need to leave tomorrow morning. I don't trust him or his armed friends.'

'He gives me the creeps, and Mayukh, what were you thinking? You were about to tell him about Abhi!'

Mayukh apologised to Swati. He realised that revealing that Abhi had been bitten might well have caused them to be turned out.

Swati and Hina went in to start the herculean task of getting

Abhi to put aside his car and sleep. Mayukh and David sat on their respective beds to take stock of their situation.

'Mayukh, I agree with Hina. We need to leave first thing tomorrow morning.'

'We don't have a car anymore.'

David knew that, and hated the fact that they had such few options. Unable to think of a solution, they finally went to bed, but Mayukh found it impossible to sleep.

At midnight, he stepped out, feeling the chill in the air, and saw that Swati was sitting on the porch of the adjoining villa. He walked over.

'Couldn't sleep either?'

As he sat down next to her, she reached out and held him tight, somewhat to his surprise.

'I'm sorry I snapped at you earlier.'

'Hey, I was stupid to talk about Abhi. It's cool. Really.'

They sat like that for some time, savouring being alone, when they were not sharing a room with others, or on the watch for attackers. As it got a bit colder, they cuddled closer, and Mayukh reached down to raise Swati's face. He looked into her eyes, wondering how this girl had come to mean so much to him in such a short period of time. He was about to kiss her when he heard a loud boom.

David rushed out, his pistol in hand and his rifle slung across his back. He looked at Mayukh and shouted, 'That was a gunshot!'

Mayukh ran just steps behind David towards the main gate.

He had asked Swati to lock the door and stay inside their villa with Hina and Abhi, not really sure what was going on. As they ran, they heard several more shots.

They spotted Walter and Mikhail, perched on a raised platform near the main gate, both firing at something, or someone, outside the gates. David climbed up the platform, followed by Mayukh, who was having trouble keeping up with the soldier.

What David saw stopped him cold. Outside the gate, several Biters were burning, lying entangled in electric wires that had been strewn around the complex, and a few that were standing were being cut to ribbons by the withering blasts from shotguns that were sending multiple pellets out at the Biters.

Mayukh looked at Walter and was instantly struck with a fear that he had never felt before, even when he had been trying to escape the Biters. Walter's lips were pursed back, his smile long gone, and his teeth bared, almost like an animal on the hunt. He was shouting as he fired.

'Burn, baby, burn!'

David heard some of the Biters scream in defiance, but when all but a few were burnt or cut down, the others retreated into the shadows. Walter stood there panting heavily, and then realising that he was not alone, his smile returned, his face transforming in an instant. The genteel, friendly Walter was back. Only his intense, focused eyes indicated the kind of violence he had just shown himself capable of.

'Captain, they come every night, and the same thing happens. Buggers don't learn.'

As they walked down, David wondered how to broach the

subject and then decided that playing it straight was the only way he knew how to.

'Walter, I have something to ask you. Electrified perimeter fences, Mossberg shotguns that certainly aren't available for public sale in India, and the way you and your friend were shooting. You don't look and act like holidaying businessmen who were caught up in this situation.'

Walter paused in midstride and turned to look at David. His cold, calculating expression at once told David that he had made a mistake in laying out his questions quite so bluntly.

'Captain, *I* do not know how a fully armed US Navy SEAL ended up in downtown Delhi, nor do I care to know. We are where we are, and the more we focus on keeping those damn Biters away and not interrogating each other, the better off we will be.'

Walter was about to storm off when he turned.

'And it's no mystery as to how they can be killed. TV, phones and the internet may be off, but ham radio operators are everywhere, and news spreads fast. We learnt early that they burn and that once you blow them up, they stay that way. That's why we use only shotguns. Of course, with useful intelligence come useless rumours, like the talk about Muslims spreading the infection that Sharma and some of his friends have taken to heart.'

Walter and Mikhail walked off, and Mayukh looked at David, whose face was an inscrutable mask.

'David, what happened? Pissed you off that much, did he?'

David leaned against the platform and looked at Mayukh, his eyes filled with concern.

'Mayukh, I never told him or the swami that I ended up in Delhi. If they have learnt so much about the Biters and perhaps us from radio operators, what have they learnt about Abhi?'

Mayukh returned to their villa, while David said that he would stay by the gate. He was worried sick by what David had just said, and it brought home to him just how important it was for him to deliver Abhi and Swati to safety. For much of his life, he had been told, perhaps fairly enough, by his parents, that he never took any of his responsibilities seriously. But now, he had a very real responsibility towards the girl he thought he was beginning to fall in love with, and the little bundle of energy that was Abhi. Knowing that they depended on him made the burden of his responsibility almost too much for him to bear. Yes, David was there, but at the end of the day, he knew that he was the one who would be most gutted if anything at all happened to Swati or Abhi. And he was not at all sure he would be able to protect them.

He spotted Swami Vinesh outside Swati and Hina's villa. Mayukh broke into a run and caught up with the swami just as he was coming out of the gate leading to the main door. In the light of the torch that was lit nearby, Mayukh saw that the swami seemed startled when he reached him, panting slightly from the sprint.

'Hello. What brings you here this late?'

Mayukh realised that perhaps he was imagining things, being paranoid, or quite possibly both, but the swami seemed a bit irritated at his question. His suspicion was confirmed when the swami snapped back.

'Do I need permission to visit them?'

Mayukh almost lost his temper, but forced to keep himself calm. There was nothing to be gained by seeking out a confrontation this late at night, when there was no way they could survive outside the swami's complex. Yet, he wanted to convey to the swami that he was not just a boy to be brushed away lightly. The swami was lean and wiry, much like Mayukh, but Mayukh had at least three to four inches on him. So he stepped closer, towering over the swami.

'No, you don't need my permission. This is your complex, but we are together, so it is most certainly my business if someone lurks outside their villa this late at night.'

He looked straight into the swami's eyes, not blinking or flinching, till the swami averted his eyes and walked off without a word. Something told Mayukh that the swami was a dangerous man to humiliate, but he was now beyond caring.

He walked to the door of the villa and knocked on it gently. Swati opened the door and both she and Hina came out.

'Abhi's fast asleep. Only a small child could sleep through gunfire,' Hina said with a smile.

Mayukh updated them on what had happened and asked if the swami had met them.

They looked puzzled, and Hina said, 'That's strange. He didn't even knock on the door. What was he doing here snooping around this late?'

They sat down on the porch.

'How are we going to get out of here and reach Ladakh? We don't have a car, and I doubt the swami will lend us one.'

'Maybe he will,' Mayukh said, with more optimism than he felt.

'Mayukh, I don't like the feel of this place at all. The swami has always had a bad reputation, and Walter and his friends are clearly not who they claim they are. Also, the reaction that Sharma character had to my being Muslim was horrible. It all feels very creepy.'

Swati had been quiet till now. When she spoke, her uncertain tone gave away just how worried she was. 'I would love to believe that we're safe here, but I'm really freaked out. I spoke to a few of the other people when the swami was giving his lecture. Most are his die-hard followers, and believe in him blindly—it's like a cult. The others are poor villagers from nearby who are just happy to be alive.'

Suddenly they heard what sounded like a large number of firecrackers going off all at once.

'What's that?' exclaimed Hina.

'That's automatic weapon fire, and it's coming from the main gate. David's there all alone, and all he has is his pistol!'

With that, Mayukh ran towards the main gate at full speed.

David was crouched on the platform, ducking behind the wall. Walter and three other men were with him, firing away occasionally with their shotguns, but more often than not, ducking like David.

Mayukh knew that David had no ammunition left for his rifle, yet he had his rifle on his shoulder and was peering through the scope. As he came closer, he realised what was going on. David was using the night vision on his scope to guide Walter and the others in shooting at whoever was firing from the outside.

Mayukh climbed up the platform, but before he could say anything, David shoved him down.

'Keep your head down. They have automatic weapons!'

Mayukh wondered who could be attacking them with automatic weapons, but didn't want to distract the men with his questions. David kept popping his head up, scoping out a target and then Walter and his friends would blast away with their shotguns till the target was neutralised. There was heavy firing coming from outside the wall, but as far as Mayukh could make out, not a single bullet came even close to hitting the wall, let alone the men gathered on the platform. The attackers were either atrocious shots, or had no idea what they were doing.

The firing subsided after about ten minutes, and David yelled out to Walter, 'Stop wasting ammo! They're all wasted or have run away!'

The men stopped firing, and Mayukh saw that something had fundamentally changed in the group dynamics. For all his earlier bluster, Walter looked shaken, and was taking orders from David.

'Captain, I'll go let the swami know what happened.'

As the others walked off, Mayukh looked at David, who was still scanning the area beyond the gate.

'What happened to him? He was ready to salute you, I think. Also, who the hell was shooting at us?'

David put his gun aside and turned towards Mayukh.

'I don't know his story, but I'll bet he has some military experience. However, shooting zombies from a safe distance is one thing, being shot at with automatic weapons is another. I think big Mikhail there pissed his pants.'

Mayukh laughed but then realised that David was dead serious.

'As for who was shooting at us, it was the damn Biters.'

A chill went down Mayukh's spine. The Biters had been evolving, but so far the most he had seen them do was throw rocks. If Purohit's theory was correct, and they were remembering common memories from the origin of the infection in Afghanistan, was it possible that they had learnt how to use weapons?

David clapped Mayukh on his shoulder.

'They can't aim to save their lives and were just spraying in the sky. But it's probably just a matter of time before they remember or learn how to use the guns effectively.'

Mayukh didn't even want to contemplate what would happen when that came to pass.

Even though the rest of the night passed without incident, none of them had slept a wink. They went into Hina's villa, and David sat by the door, pistol in hand.

Sometime before sunrise, Abhi woke up and was quite confused to see all the adults sitting around, looking so serious. He turned to Swati.

'Are you happy?'

She couldn't help but laugh and assured him that they were all happy. Then, a look of concern came over his face.

'Where is McQueen?'

Mayukh fished out the red car from under a bed, and passed it to Abhi, who immediately began playing with it, oblivious to the worries that were gnawing away at the others.

Mayukh stepped out at about eight in the morning, and saw some of the ashram's residents walking about. All of them seemed to be moving quickly, as if in a hurry to finish whatever work they had and then get back to the perceived safety of their villas. He saw Sharma walking along the road, and called out to him.

'Mr Sharma, what's Swami Vinesh doing? We'd like to have a word with him.'

Sharma just nodded and continued on his way. Mayukh was beginning to wonder whether Sharma had passed on the message when ten minutes later, Swami Vinesh came to the villa himself. He looked haggard, and his sharp eyes were ringed with dark circles.

When he was inside, he first addressed David. 'You are the military man here. If those Biters can indeed learn to fire guns, what are our chances?'

'Swami, the short answer is zero. You have a handful of armed men, and honestly, though they haven't told me who they really are, they seem to have some experience in the military. But it was easy when the Biters were launching themselves into the electrified fence and standing about, waiting to be shot to pieces. If they can learn to shoot straight, then it's just a matter of time before your guards are dead and they come over. All it requires is for them to develop the sense to run a vehicle through the fence and break a part of it.'

The swami seemed to crumple on David's reply. He mulled his answer before saying it out loud.

'Walter and his friends were soldiers in the Russian and Eastern Bloc armies, and later became arms dealers. They peddled Eastern European small arms to anybody who had the money. Walter became my devotee a year ago, and they were here both for the meditation and to meet some clients about their shotguns.'

David's face showed his disgust. For a professional soldier, there was nothing worse than a gun runner who sold weapons in the black market, which all too often ended up in the hands of terrorists.

The swami got up to leave when Hina stopped him.

'We are thankful for the shelter you gave us, but we must be on our way. If we leave now, we may be able make it to Ladakh by nightfall. Do you know if there are any running vehicles in the neighbouring villages? I'm sure lots of tourists would have driven here.'

To their relief and surprise, the swami said he would get Sharma and his staff to rustle up a car that was in running condition and had enough fuel, adding that if they left within the hour, they could get to Ladakh by nightfall.

When he left, Swati commented with a smile, 'Now that was easier than I thought it would be. Maybe he just looks creepier than he is.'

With everyone's mood considerably lightened, they began to make preparations for their journey. They unloaded all their remaining supplies from Walter's van and piled them up near the gate, ready to be loaded into whatever vehicle Sharma managed to find for them.

Forty-five minutes later, there was still no sign of Sharma or a car. Mayukh glanced at his watch and said he would go over to the swami's villa and check what was going on.

At the swami's villa, Mayukh knocked twice, and hearing

no response, peeped in through an open window to see that it was empty. He figured his best bet was to go to the administrative office and see if he could find Sharma or the swami there.

As he approached the office, he saw Sharma walking out of it, smoking a cigarette.

'Mr Sharma, did you find the car the swami asked you to get for us?'

Sharma fumbled with his cigarette, almost dropping it in surprise on being accosted by Mayukh. He just shook his head and rushed away before Mayukh could ask him anything else.

Suspecting that something was amiss, Mayukh was about to storm into the office, when he heard raised voices inside. He peered in through the open door, and saw the swami and Walter talking.

'Walter, you've seen the damn piece of paper as well! It's clear what they want. Let them have the boy and maybe they'll leave us alone.'

'Look, Vinesh, they are goddamned mindless zombies! We've killed dozens every night. Let them come again and we can hold them off.'

'Oh yes, we have held them off when they were walking in blind. But now they can shoot! Don't you get it? They can think. They can write. They can shoot. They can't do any of these things as well as us, but they are learning. How long before they break in here and turn us into creatures like them? No, no, actually, they won't do that. You've heard from the radio broadcasts what they do to those who try and fight.'

Walter looked deflated and sat down.

'He's only a boy, Vinesh. Also, if we do hand him over, what guarantee is there that they'll leave us alone?'

'I know, but what choice do we have? When the Biters tossed the paper over the wall during their first attack, I went to their villa, thinking I could take the boy then. But I couldn't bring myself to do it. Then they came back with automatic weapons—as if to warn us. There are no guarantees that they'll leave us alone, but I can guarantee that they will tear us all to shreds if we don't do what they say.'

Mayukh's heart was already pounding with what he had overheard, but when he saw the bloodied piece of paper in the swami's hand, he was terrified. The swami was brandishing the paper in the air, as if demonstrating that what was on it sealed his point. Scrawled in large red letters, as if written with blood by a child who had just learnt to write, were three words: *Gives the boye.*

Mayukh turned to warn the others, when he saw Mikhail standing behind him. Before he could do anything, the big man shoved him into the office.

Swami Vinesh and Walter looked at him in shock and then at each other. Seeing the outrage and anger in Mayukh's eyes, they knew that he had overheard their conversation. The swami walked up to Mayukh, even now trying to be his usual smooth self.

'Mayukh, we don't have a choice. If we give them the boy, we can all live. So many lives have already been lost. One boy could save us all.'

Mayukh got up unsteadily to his feet and waited for the swami to get closer. Then he put all his strength into a kick right into the swami's groin.

The swami doubled over with a scream and fell to his knees, as Walter struck Mayukh with a blow to the head with the butt of his pistol. Mayukh found himself flat on the ground, his head spinning and warm blood beginning to stream down his face. He tried to get up, but Mikhail kicked him in the stomach, sending him down again, his body wracked with pain.

He heard the swami shout, 'Go get the boy! And kill the soldier if you have to!'

Mayukh tried to get up again, but his legs felt like jelly and he fell again. He saw Walter looking down at him, grinning, and then lashing out with his leg towards Mayukh's head.

Mayukh saw no more.

TEN

Hina crawled along the side of the wall, wary of making any noise. It was almost five in the evening, and from what she had heard, Abhi was to be handed over as soon as the sun set. She knew she had less than an hour in which to do something about it. The problem was that being an old college professor and closet novelist meant that she had little by way of the practical skills such a situation warranted.

Hina had been in one of the communal washrooms several hours earlier when Walter and Mikhail had come running towards the gate, shouting that they had found a car that was in running condition, and that they wanted David to have a look at it before they loaded all their supplies. Swati had been playing with Abhi near the gate.

In the washroom, Hina had heard their loud voices, and had been overjoyed at the message. As she looked out of the washroom window, David had put his gun in its holster and started to walk away with them.

That was when things had gone very, very wrong.

One of Walter's men had come up behind David and hit him hard on the back of the head with the butt of his shotgun. David had staggered to the ground, bleeding from the head, but even then, he had not gone down without a fight. He had roared in anger at this betrayal and turned around and struck the man in the throat with his fist. The big man had gone down, screaming in pain. Walter and Mikhail had hit David again, this time sending him down for good. Two other men had grabbed Swati and Abhi. Swati scratched and kicked with all her strength, but it was not enough, and they were carted away.

The swami and Sharma had appeared on the scene. The swami was shouting to Walter, 'Where is that old hag? Go and find her!'

Hina had slipped out of the washroom and hidden under its slightly raised stilts for the next few hours while Walter and his henchmen searched for her. She had no idea what had happened to cause this betrayal at that time, and had been focused purely on remaining hidden. That was till she overheard the swami and Walter talking, as they passed her hideout, about handing over Abhi to the Biters.

She was old, she was weak, and she had no idea what to do, but she was sure of one thing: she could not let Abhi be sacrificed like this.

Mayukh's head was pounding with pain and his face sticky with dried blood. He could barely see out of his left eye. He wiped the blood off the left side of his face, and was able to see somewhat better.

He realised there was a sobbing noise to his right. He turned to see Swati there, looking pale and scared.

'They took Abhi!'

It all came back to Mayukh then. What he had heard at the office, the blows Mikhail and Walter had showered on him, the deal the swami thought he could strike with the Biters. He tried to speak but his throat was parched, and a mere croak escaped his lips.

Swati cradled him in her arms, and poured some water into his mouth. He drank it greedily, and then sputtered and coughed as he took in more than he should have.

He sat up. He and Swati had been locked inside the bathroom of the villa he and David had been assigned, with only a bottle of water between them. He asked where Hina and David were, but Swati merely shook her head between sobs.

The pain in his head was excruciating, but Mayukh felt something even more overpowering than the pain. Anger. A red-hot rage more intense than anything he had felt before. He was sure that if the swami or Walter had been in front of him, he would have killed them without a second thought. The problem was that he was unarmed and locked in.

He looked at his watch. There was very little time left before the swami offered up Abhi as sacrifice to the Biters in his misguided hope that they would leave him and his followers alone.

He banged on the door, shouting and kicking against it with all his strength, but it would not budge. Then he closed his eyes and forced himself to calm down, praying that some idea would occur to him.

Hina stiffened. It had sounded like Mayukh, but she could not be sure. Yet, if there was a chance that he was alive, joining him would at least make it two of them, and hopefully he would have some ideas about how to save Abhi.

She crept out of her hiding place behind the villa. The shout had seemed to come from the villa David and Mayukh had been in. Then she stopped in her tracks.

In front of the villa were seated Sharma and one of Walter's meatheads, a tall, strongly built European, cradling a shotgun. She flattened herself against the rear wall of the villa again, thinking furiously about what she could do. What the hell *could* she do?

If she had been writing a novel, what would her heroine have done? In one of her bestselling novels, *The Thuggees*, the heroine, an Indian princess, is abducted by a group of Indian bandits, and has to escape while her British lover mounts a rescue mission. The heroine makes it because her aging attendant does something the bandits don't expect her to, and that element of surprise gives the princess the chance to escape.

Of course, she had put much more time and energy into describing the romance between the princess and her British lover, but she did remember the old attendant's final charge. And now it seemed that her fiction was going to come true, though of course, she was not going to be the mesmerisingly beautiful princess but the doomed old hag. Oh well, one has to play the cards one is dealt with, she thought, and steeled herself as she walked out into the open and towards the two men.

Sharma looked at Hina walking calmly towards them, a smile on her face, and stood up, ashen-faced. The man next to him asked him what had happened and then he too stiffened on seeing Hina walk towards them, humming a song, as if oblivious to the fate that had befallen her friends.

Hina's heart was pounding. Every ounce of common sense in her told her to run and hide, but somehow she pushed that aside and kept walking calmly towards the two men, with a broad smile on her face.

'Hello, Mr Sharma!'

David couldn't believe what he was seeing. Hina had either completely lost her mind or was about to perform the most awesomely stupid act of bravery he had ever seen. He had been lying under the next villa, covered in mud, hiding in plain sight for the last ten minutes, waiting for the moment to make his move. He knew that he would have a tough time taking on Walter and his men alone, unarmed, and with his left hand broken, but if he managed to get Mayukh out, they might stand a chance.

He had no sensation in the fingers of his left hand, which Mikhail had stomped to a pulp with his heavy hiking boots. David couldn't be sure, but he reckoned that at least three of his fingers were broken and that his left shoulder had been popped out of its socket.

He had been woken up when water was splashed on his face, and had found himself in a villa, with his hands and feet tied, and with Mikhail raging at him about how he had killed his best friend. That was when David had remembered the betrayal at the gate and the big man whose thorax he had crushed before he had been brought down.

He had looked into Mikhail's eyes and was sure that the big man would kill him; he had been ready to face his death when Mikhail had brought up his shotgun. But then Mikhail had decided to have some sport first and beat David with the butt of his gun and had then broken his fingers.

Apparently satisfied with the damage he had caused, Mikhail had raised his gun to finish the job when Walter had come in and screamed at him to stop. When Mikhail had said something about David having killed Matthau, Walter told him he could have his revenge after the boy was handed over, but for now, he needed to prepare the defences for the evening, and get one of his men to guard Mayukh and Swati at the villa. Enraged, Mikhail kicked David's prone body a few more times. Though wracked with pain, David's training made him still his mind, try to block out the pain and pretend to have passed out. He heard Walter tell Mikhail that David was half-dead anyway, and then the two of them had left.

David had lain still till he heard the door being locked. Then he had really passed out from the pain, and had come to only hours later.

Which is when he began to plot. For all their tough talk and muscle, Mikhail and his cronies were hardly the worst he had faced. He had lived through Hell Week in SEAL training, where nine out of ten of the toughest soldiers in the world dropped out; he had fought hand-to-hand with Al-Qaeda fanatics in Afghanistan, and had killed more men in combat than he cared to remember. He had only one good hand, and his head was still bleeding, and it was likely he had concussion. But Captain David Bremsak was going to war again, and this time it was personal.

In ten minutes, he had undone the ropes binding him and picked the lock on the door. There had been no guard outside, perhaps because Walter had thought him to be incapacitated. That was a wrong assumption that David would make him pay dearly for.

Seeing the guard outside the villa where Mayukh and Swati were being held, he had hidden and waited for the right opportunity to make his move, trying to figure out how he could take the guard out despite having no weapon and only one good hand. He had half smiled when he thought that, for all the crap the movies showed about Navy SEALs, he honestly had no clue what to do.

He had seen Sharma come over, and overheard them talk about what was to come. When he heard what was being planned for Abhi, a red mist of rage came over him, and broken hand and concussion notwithstanding, he told himself that Walter and the swami would be dead men before the night ended. He had been wondering how to make his move when Hina started walking towards the men, humming a song and cheerfully greeting them.

He crawled forward using his good hand, and readied himself for action.

‘Can the bitch really not know what's going on?'

The man next to Sharma didn't answer because he was as

confused by Hina's sudden appearance. Hina was now just a couple of feet away, and was singing loudly.

'Let her come closer and then we'll grab her. We can just lock her in with the others, and let the swami decide what to do with them after we're finished with getting the boy to the Biters.'

The European lowered his shotgun so he would look less threatening and took a step toward Hina, smiling back at her.

'Would you like to meet your friends?'

Hina smiled cheerily and said, 'Of course! Can you show me where they are?'

The man took another step forward, convinced that the old woman had lost her mind and extended his right arm towards her. Hina took it with her left arm and seemed to trip on something and fall forward. The man dropped his shotgun in trying to support her.

That was when Hina brought her right hand out from behind her and slammed the fist-sized rock she was clutching into the side of the man's head with all the strength she could muster.

The man went down, screaming in pain, clutching at his bloodied face.

Hina looked up, readying to handle Sharma. To her shock, far from attacking her, he squealed in fright and turned to run.

Hina's hand was ringing from the impact of the blow she had delivered, but she brought her hand up again and delivered another blow to the kneeling man's head. He did not get back up.

Sharma was now backed up against the villa, and Hina

picked up the fallen man's shotgun. She had no idea how to use it, but the violence she had just dished out had taken all the fight out of Sharma, who was now pleading with her to spare him.

'You bastard, open the door and let them out first!'

Sharma went into the villa, pushed along by Hina at the point of the gun, and opened the bathroom door.

Mayukh started in surprise as the door swung open and he saw Sharma there, and then Hina behind him, shotgun in hand.

She smiled when she saw them. 'Now you young people can join the fun.'

Sharma looked at Hina.

'Please let me go. I have nothing to do with the swami and Walter's plan.'

Swati was on him like a tiger; she slapped him so hard he fell against the wall.

'You fucking animal! You're going to kill a small boy to save yourselves!'

Mayukh held Sharma by his neck and head-butted him as hard as he could. He heard the thin man's nose snap, and then Sharma crumpled to the floor.

Mayukh locked him in the bathroom and the three of them hugged. Hina's bravado was now gone and she was shaking uncontrollably. But now, they all knew that they had to put their fears and weaknesses aside and try and save Abhi.

As they stepped out of the villa, they found Mikhail standing there, a shotgun pointed towards them.

'Put the gun down!'

Hina did as she was told, in large measure because the gun was anyway useless in her hands.

Mikhail looked at the man lying on the ground, a small pool of blood forming around his head. Hina followed his gaze and she felt nauseous at the thought that she may have killed a man.

Mikhail looked up at them. Spittle flew towards them as he screamed furiously, 'I should have killed all of you!'

He strode towards them. Mayukh stepped in front of the women.

Mikhail hit him hard on the side of the head with the butt of his gun, sending him down.

Mikhail brought his shotgun up to fire at Mayukh's prone figure when his legs gave way under him and he went down himself.

David kicked the shotgun away, knowing he could not use it with one hand, and then faced Mikhail.

Mayukh saw David's bloodied face and his left hand hanging uselessly by his side and stepped forward to help, but David waved him back. Swati, Hina and Mayukh watched their bloodied and battered friend face off against the giant before him.

'I should have killed you when I had the chance,' Mikhail said as he reached for the handgun tucked into his waist.

David moved so fast that Mikhail barely had time to register his actions. A kick shattered Mikhail's femur and as he hollered in pain and grabbed his leg, David struck out with the open palm of his right hand against the bigger man's nose. They heard a crunching noise as Mikhail's nose broke and the crushed bones were pushed back inside towards his brain. Mikhail was dead before his body hit the ground.

David stood over him and murmured, 'Yes, you should have.'

He looked at the others, and felt something that he had not felt in some time. The intense pride, almost love, a combat soldier feels for the mates fighting next to him, willing to die for each other. He could not have had an unlikelier group to go to war with—a young girl, a schoolboy and an old woman—but right then, he would have chosen them over a platoon of SEALs. He stepped forward and they rushed towards him, and for a minute they just stood there, holding one another, aware of just how close the last few days had brought them.

Then they heard a crescendo of howling. The sun had set and the Biters had come out.

Just a day ago, they would have hidden in the dark, trying to keep themselves alive, but now they just looked at one another, an unspoken consensus on what needed to be done, no matter what it meant for their own lives and safety.

Mayukh said what was on everyone's mind. 'Let's go get the little guy.'

Swami Vinesh shivered despite the fact that he was wearing a thick coat over his saffron robes. Looking at the dozens, possibly hundreds, of Biters gathered outside the ashram walls, he knew that it was not the cold that was causing the shivering.

The torches along the walls had all been lit, and in the darkness, they cast a faint glow over the gathering horde outside. He tried not to look, but could not help himself. The ghouls gathered outside could have been people he had met in the local market just a week ago, or even people who had come to his ashram seeking instant salvation. Their clothes seemed to indicate that they came from all sorts of backgrounds.

He saw a tall, thin man, or rather the remains of what used to be a man, dressed in a tattered suit, his tie still around his neck, standing right next to a yellowing, decaying woman who was dressed in rags, of the sort beggars on the roadside wore. Swami Vinesh looked on in mortified horror, wondering if the plague or infection or whatever it had been, had been the great equalizer after all. Men, women, rich, poor—all brought together by a mindless blood lust, and yes, those damned black turbans.

The swami had no idea whether the legend of the boy being immune to the Biters was true or not, as some of the half-crazed radio broadcasts claimed, nor did he know how the Biters had found out. He had heard of all the stories and had heard of the group with the boy setting out from Delhi in an SUV. When Walter had chanced upon them, he had considered finding out whether the legend was true and whether that would give him any bargaining power with whatever authorities claimed to still be in control in Ladakh. Before the outbreak, he had been on the verge of disgrace and imprisonment; now he saw a chance to reinvent himself as a saviour and hero.

But then, the Biters had arrived on the scene, apparently

aware the boy was with them, asking for him, and now suddenly able to fire guns. How the Biters knew of the boy was beyond him. Was it possible that some of those who had learnt of the boy and then got infected had retained the memory?

Walter poked him in the shoulder.

'Vinesh, this is not a good time to go soft. Vineet has the kid just below and we know the Biters mean business.'

Walter had in his hand a crumpled note that had been tied to a rock and tossed over the wall a short while before. It read, *Gives boye you lives.*

Swami Vinesh looked down below the platform to see Vineet trying to hold onto Abhi. The little boy had proved to be more than a handful. Walter was still sore where Abhi had bitten him on the forearm, and he had pulled Sharma's hair so hard the man had actually cried. But he was a little boy, a boy whom the swami was about to hand over to the mob outside.

'Walter, give me a minute. I need to ... prepare.'

Walter snorted derisively as he understood just what the man meant.

The swami hurried back to his villa, meeting several of his disciples lounging around the ashram, most with glazed eyes and vacuous smiles. He went into his villa and lit up a joint, inhaling deeply. After his second joint, he was feeling lightheaded enough to contemplate carrying out what he needed to do.

As he was about to leave his villa, he saw a woman sleeping in a corner. He tried to remember her name, but it wasn't important—another young devotee who had wanted to believe in someone, or something, so bad that she was willing to bed him for it. The marijuana he used to spike the food and drink served to all his visiting devotees certainly helped.

When times had been good, that had made people go away light-headed and feeling instantly better, and he picked up more devotees. It helped that Manali was a major hub for the drug trade and the likes of Walter peddled more than just guns. Now, with the threat of the Biters outside, extra doses meant that his hardcore devotees were ever more hooked to him and his offerings. Of all the dirty secrets that supposedly existed about Swami Vinesh, he chuckled as he wondered what the press would have made of this one. Oh well, it no longer mattered. Now, it was just a case of keeping himself alive as long as he could.

Swati and Mayukh had been moving slowly behind the cover of the villas when they spotted Abhi. Swati almost broke from Mayukh's grasp and ran as she saw her brother in Vineet's hands, and he had to struggle to hold her back.

'Swati, I know how you feel, but we cannot just rush in. There are four armed men there.'

Swati subsided, but her eyes remained fiery with rage as they started to put their plan into motion.

The swami was back on the platform, looking down at

the Biters, who unlike their mad rushes of the past, were standing well clear of the electrified fence. Looking at the yellowed, bloodied faces looking up at him with lifeless eyes, the swami could not discern any sign of humanity, let alone intelligence, yet the Biters were obviously evolving.

That point was made most clearly when three Biters stepped in front of the crowd. They were all tall and well built, and the swami could see them wearing the tattered remains of what had once been police uniforms. All three carried automatic rifles, which they were pointing in the general direction of the ashram. When they stepped forward, the mob started howling—a keening, high-pitched sound that made the swami want to cover his ears.

One of the armed Biters took one step forward and pointed up at the swami, and screamed just one word.

Boy!

A dozen feet behind them, David crouched behind a villa, watching. His left arm was now numb, though it had hurt like hell when he had forced his shoulder back into its socket. Since he could not hope to use a shotgun effectively, he had taken Mikhail's pistol, an old Makarov that still seemed to be in good condition.

Their hastily concocted plan had been set in motion. Mayukh and Swati were to gather as many of their provisions as possible and load them into Walter's van, which Hina was to drive. David would lead the assault, and Mayukh would back him up, with Swati for added cover.

David smiled to himself as he contemplated their chances. Walter and the three men with him were armed with shotguns, and seemed to know how to use them. For all he knew, the swami could be armed as well. That left them facing at least four armed men, and hundreds of Biters, an unknown number of them now armed with automatic weapons.

David's army, as it were, consisted of a one-armed commando, a boy with a weapon that he had never fired before, a girl who did not know how to unlock the safety on her pistol, and an old romance novelist to drive their getaway car.

Mayukh and Swati edged closer to the platform, hidden behind another villa about fifty metres from David's hiding place. They had been able to find most of their winter clothing in Sharma's office, a disclosure the man readily made when Mayukh threatened to break something else other than his nose. However, all their food and provisions had been stored with the ashram's stocks, and with many of the swami's disciples hovering around the villas that were used for food storage, they could not risk trying to get them.

Mayukh hefted the shotgun in his hands, feeling its weight. He had never fired one before, and despite David's five-minute tutorial, he was not sure he would be able to do much with it. The other shotgun they had recovered was slung behind his back. Swati had a pistol in her hands, which she was trying hard to keep from shaking. They were both terrified, yet they were more determined to do this than they had ever been about anything. That stemmed from the little boy who now stood just a dozen feet in front of them.

Vineet, holding Abhi, was cursing the boy after being bitten yet again. He wondered where his boss, Sharma, was. Figuring he was either hiding or asleep, he cursed having to be a part of this. He wanted to live of course, but he was not sure he liked the idea of having to hand over a kid to the Biters.

'Vineet, give him to me!'

Vineet lifted Abhi up and Walter grabbed the boy, holding him above his head. The Biters seemed to quiet down, their howling reduced to a murmur. As Walter kept Abhi raised, the swami took one of the lit torches nearby and held it close to Abhi's legs. Abhi now saw the horde of Biters assembled below and began crying and screaming in terror, but his voice was drowned out by the howling that soon began among the Biters when they saw him. Some of the Biters, no longer able to control themselves, surged forward and were instantly caught in the electrified fence, where they lay twitching and smoking. The others stepped back immediately, but continued howling and screaming. The two men with Walter kept their shotguns trained on the Biters, but Walter could see them begin to lose their nerve. He knew they had to end this soon.

'Vinesh, should I just throw the boy to them?'

The swami seemed transfixed by the mob of Biters below

him. He looked towards Walter, his face blank, and took out another joint.

Walter shouted at him, 'Vinesh, come on!'

'Do it!'

Walter leaned towards the wall, and held his hands back, readying himself to throw Abhi into the crowd below. He didn't know if he would be able to clear the fence, and he didn't care. There was little chance the boy would survive the fall, and he hoped that would be enough to satisfy the Biters.

As he raised Abhi to hurl him, a bullet hit his left calf, sending him staggering forward, dropping Abhi onto the platform. He grabbed his leg, screaming at his men to get whoever had shot him. Both men now turned towards the inside of the ashram, scanning for attackers. One of them saw a figure moving to the left and fired.

David felt some of the shotgun pellets pass close by, perhaps even grazing him, but from thirty or more metres away, it was going to be difficult to score a direct hit with a shotgun. On the other hand, he could easily hit his targets with his pistol. The problem was his left hand was useless, and with fatigue and pain beginning to catch up with him, he was hardly moving as fast as he could.

Another shotgun blast rang out from the platform as David dived behind a fence that shattered as the pellets hit it. David screamed in agony as he landed on his left hand. He turned towards the platform. Knowing Abhi was there, he could not fire indiscriminately, so he steadied his aim, ignoring the pain shooting through his left side and fired twice.

One of the men next to Walter spun and fell, and the other dived for the ground.

'You idiot! Get him!'

But now it was every man for himself. Swami Vinesh had been snapped back to reality by the shooting, and his eyes were now crazed with fear and despair.

'Walter, throw the boy!'

But it was too late for that.

The Biters surged forward as one, screaming louder than ever, enraged by what they perhaps saw as a betrayal. The first few were caught in the wires and burnt where they lay, but others clambered over their burning bodies. Several of them were carrying firearms and a steady volley of rifle and pistol fire soon reached out towards the ashram.

Walter ducked behind the wall, unslinging his own shotgun. He kicked at his remaining man, shouting at him to get up and shoot. The man stood up and was scanning the area for David when he was hit by a bullet from behind. The Biters must have fired hundreds of rounds blindly, but this one round struck home, sending the man down.

David clambered out of cover and ran towards the platform, firing at Walter, who returned fire with his shotgun. At closer range, he nicked David, who went down on one knee, grabbing his shoulder. Walter was about to deliver the killing shot when Mayukh barrelled into him.

In the midst of the firefight, none of them had noticed Mayukh climbing onto the platform. He could not risk firing the shotgun with Abhi around in close proximity, so he put the shotgun to the next best use.

As Walter kicked him away and tried to get up, Mayukh swung his shotgun like a club, catching Walter squarely on the side of his head. There was a sharp cracking sound as the shotgun's butt smashed into his skull. Walter dropped and lay unmoving on the platform.

Mayukh grabbed Abhi and was about to climb down when he crossed paths with the swami. The swami was unarmed, but his face was contorted with rage.

'You fools! Now they will kill us all!'

He tried to grab Abhi, but Mayukh kicked him, all his anger and desperation going into the blow that sent the swami sprawling.

Mayukh began to climb down the ladder that led to the platform. He could hear the Biters now pounding away at the main gate of the ashram. It was but a matter of time before the sheer weight of their numbers would win and they would be inside the ashram.

Mayukh suddenly felt a tug and looked up to see the swami pulling on Abhi's arm. The boy was screaming in terror and pain and Mayukh realised that hanging from the ladder with one arm and trying to hold onto Abhi with the other, he had little chance of winning this tug-of-war.

The swami abruptly fell back as if he had been struck and did not get up, and a split second later Mayukh heard two blasts close to his ear. He looked over his shoulder to see Swati standing near the foot of the platform, raised pistol in hand. He clambered down, and Swati gathered her little brother in her arms as they waited for the final part of their plan.

The gate of the ashram was now beginning to give way and Mayukh saw one or two yellowed hands appear through cracks in the gate. David came up to them, and Mayukh wondered just how badly David had been wounded. His left hand was still hanging limply by his side, and the right side of his torso seemed to be covered in blood.

He was distracted from saying anything by the sight of several of the swami's devotees running for the gate in sheer mad panic. He wondered if they had not realised that the Biters were at the gate, but it was too late to do anything for them.

The gate gave way with a mighty crash and Biters clambered over one another to enter. Two devotees closest to the gate were set upon by a dozen Biters. They were now not biting to infect, but ripping and tearing to kill.

Swati picked Abhi up in one arm, and kept the pistol in her other hand. Mayukh pumped the shotgun back as David had taught him and stepped between them and the Biters. David was by his side, holding his pistol up.

Two Biters spotted them and rushed towards them. David fired till his clip was empty, and hit one of them in the head, sending him down. The other, a short, fat man who in his undead state was moving far faster than he would ever have been capable of in life, ran straight towards Mayukh, screaming through sharp yellowed teeth, his black turban half falling off his head, where clumps of black hair were just visible in the fading light.

Mayukh steadied himself and fired, the loud blast almost deafening him and the recoil rocking him back a step. The Biter was thrown back several feet, almost cut in half by the powerful blast. To make sure, Mayukh pumped the shotgun again and fired.

But now, they had run out of time. Many more Biters were now in the compound and had encircled them. Two of them, armed with rifles, were now firing them repeatedly in the air, the rifles doing little more than clicking on empty. Evidently the Biters still hadn't learnt or remembered how to reload.

Mayukh moved closer to Swati as they readied themselves for the final onslaught. Just then, Walter's van smashed into the nearest Biters, scattering them.

Hina was at the wheel, screaming. 'Get inside now!'

They scrambled into the back as the van drove towards the gate, crushing anyone in its path.

Hina looked up to see Walter standing near the gate, pistol in hand, aiming at the van. He fired at least three times, and the windshield shattered in front of her. Without slowing down, she passed him as he dived out of the way, only to be engulfed by a mass of screaming Biters.

The van sped out of the ashram, into the uncertainty of the night.

ELEVEN

THEY DROVE in silence for several minutes.

Swati held Abhi tight to her chest, painfully aware of just how close she had come to losing him, and also dealing with the fact that she had just shot dead another human being.

David had moved to the front passenger seat, and was keeping a lookout for Biters. But he felt more naked and vulnerable than he ever had, without his night vision, without his weapons, and with one hand useless. For all his training and conditioning, this was as close to breaking point as he had ever come. It was perhaps the first time that he seriously began to doubt he would ever get back to his Rose again.

Mayukh was numb from the sudden and ferocious violence they had faced the previous day, and also filled with dread for what the night would bring. The last time he had been in a car in the night was with his mother, and remembering what had happened that night made him feel even worse.

The unlikely pillar of strength for the group turned out to be Hina. She kept up an incessant chatter, joking with Abhi, getting David to focus on trying to read road signs in the darkness, ensuring that Mayukh kept a watch out for Biters since he was the only one who could use a shotgun. They did not have any of the guides or maps with them anymore, but Hina broadly remembered the way they needed to go, and she kept pestering Mayukh and the others to confirm that she had remembered it right.

'Mayukh, we turn right on this road to stay on course for the Rohtang Pass, right?'

'Mayukh, damn it! Focus and tell me what you remember.'

'Swati, it'll get colder at night. Make sure Abhi's got an extra layer of clothing on!'

David looked at Hina with a mixture of admiration and awe. In the ashram, he had seen the raw physical courage she was capable of, and now he was seeing her take charge with more authority than the toughest trainer he'd known in Hell Week. And it was working. She was managing to get everyone to snap out of their worries, and to focus on where they were and what needed to be done.

In the darkness, Hina could barely see a few feet ahead of her, but not wanting to attract unwanted attention, she had kept the headlights off. That was till she suddenly felt the van listing to its right.

'Holy shit!'

David was more shocked by her outburst than by the van's movement.

'That's the first time I've heard you swear. What's wrong?'

Hina backed up and turned the headlights on to discover that they had been about to drive off the edge of the road. With the sharp turns and high mountain roads, she figured it was better to risk attracting Biters than to drive off a cliff. No sooner had she switched on the headlights, than Swati shouted out from the back.

'I see two of them!'

Mayukh followed her outstretched hand and he saw two

Biters less than ten feet away, just ahead of the van, lit up by the headlights. The Biters seemed as surprised to see them, and they raised their hands to their eyes as the headlights hit them.

Hina stepped on the gas and sped towards them, and they all felt the bumps as they ran over the Biters and sped on. It was a sign of just how much all of them had changed that not one of them flinched when they ran over the Biters.

It was now just past midnight, and they all knew that they could not just drive around all night and hope to survive attack after attack. They had to find some shelter for the night and then continue their journey when the sun rose.

They turned into a road that had a cluster of tightly-packed buildings on either side of it. As far as they could see, the houses were deserted, but there was no telling who or what might be lurking inside.

Suddenly the van lurched to a halt, and Hina slumped against the steering wheel.

'Hina, what's wrong?'

She did not answer Swati's question and David turned towards her.

'Are you feeling okay?'

She smiled at him, and for the first time since the escape from the ashram, he got a good look at her face. She was pale, and seemed to be struggling to keep her eyes open. Mayukh reached over from the back and touched her shoulder.

'Hina, do you need a break from driving?'

Hina smiled and coughed, and David felt his heart catch in his mouth as blood trickled out of her mouth.

'Son, I think I'm done.'

David reached out to her and his hand came back slick with blood. He got out of the van and asked Mayukh to help him pull Hina out. Now they had no choice but to seek refuge in one of the buildings.

David picked a second-floor clinic and they half carried, half dragged Hina up the stairs. It was a small two-room affair, but David thought their best bet, if attacked, was to have the Biters come up a narrow passage like the one the stairs presented so they could defend it.

It was pitch black inside, so Mayukh and Swati turned on their cell phones so they could at least see what was wrong with Hina.

Her torso was covered with blood and she was now coughing loudly, blood coming out of the corners of her mouth.

'That bald bastard shot me.'

Mayukh held her hand, blinking away his tears, as the full implication of what Hina had done for them sank in.

'You knew? Yet you ...'

Hina coughed again and spoke through gritted teeth.

'Son, take care of Swati and Abhi. Promise me you and Swati will be there for each other. That would make an old trashy romance novelist rest in peace.'

David took her head on his lap, and he felt tears sting his cheeks as she addressed him.

'Abhi. He must make it. Please ...'

Those were her final words.

Swati, holding Abhi, began crying, as Mayukh sat back against the wall, tears now flowing freely from his eyes too. David had lost many good men in combat, but never had someone's death hit him quite as hard as Hina's. She had not been a professional soldier. Indeed, if anything, she was quite the antithesis. An aging novelist and professor. Yet, in her last moments, she had shown selfless courage that David was not sure even he was capable of. He cradled her head and cried.

Their mourning was cut short by noises from downstairs. Their cell phones were off in an instant and Mayukh was at the door, where he saw shapes moving up the stairs. He couldn't see much other than their darkened silhouettes, but their jerky movements gave him a pretty good idea who they were. Any doubt he had was dispelled when one of them screamed—the same ululating screech that he had now come to recognise well.

He unslung his shotgun and fired, and fired again. He kept pumping the shotgun and pulling the trigger till it clicked empty. He pulled the trigger for several seconds after he had run out of shells, his ears ringing from the blasts, trying to take out all his anger at Hina's loss on the damned Biters coming for them. He felt David behind him.

'They're gone, kid. They're gone.'

David and Mayukh moved Hina's body to the second room. They badly wanted to give her a better resting place, but the best they could do was to put a blanket on top of her. Being in a clinic had one advantage: they could tend to their wounds. David figured he needed some stitches on his head, since the wound there was still bleeding, but he made do with slathering it with antibiotic cream and bandaging it. His left hand seemed to have four broken fingers, and while he put a makeshift splint on his hand, he knew it was as good as useless. He peeled off his uniform to see that he had been grazed in at least three places by shotgun pellets, but the worst of them were surface flesh wounds which looked much worse than they were, and only needed some cleaning up and bandaging.

Mayukh's head wound was less serious, but they didn't take any chances, and bandaged him as well. They found a few bottles of drinking water and drained them, but there was no food in sight.

They were all hungry and dead tired, but none of them slept that night. They sat huddled against each other, facing the stairs, starting at every noise they heard. Abhi was between Swati and Mayukh, and to his credit, not once did he ask for milk. All of them, in their own ways, small and big, had risen to the occasion and discovered courage and the strength to carry on. Hina's sacrifice had galvanised them; they would not give up.

Abhi spoke so softly, they almost didn't hear him.

'Hina aunty is in heaven now, isn't she? Can she still hear us?'

Mayukh stroked Abhi's hand and spoke, choking with emotion as he did. 'Yes, Abhi, I think she can.'

'Then I want her to know that I love her.'

They huddled even closer, their eyes open and moist as they waited for the sun to rise.

At daybreak, the first thing they did was to take stock of what they could find in the clinic and the adjoining houses and shops that could be useful for the journey ahead. Swati found four bottles of mineral water in a house and they put them inside the van, as they did some bandages and antiseptics from the clinic.

Abhi suddenly cried out, 'Cake!'

They all gathered near him to see the broken glass windows and unhinged door of what used to be a bakery. In the display case was a single piece of cake. Mayukh felt his stomach growl and his mouth water, so he certainly couldn't blame Abhi for rushing into the room.

'Let me have a look first.'

David picked up the piece and saw that it was spoilt, green fungus appearing where vanilla icing once was.

'I'm sorry, Abhi, this isn't nice anymore.'

'But I'm so hungry!'

Swati's heart broke to see her little brother like this, but she knew David was right. The last thing they needed was for one of them to fall sick from eating spoilt food.

They got in the van, with Swati driving. With only one hand useful, David could not drive, and this left Mayukh free to use the shotgun in case they encountered a threat. They drove through meandering hill roads for at least an hour, seeing nothing but tall trees by the edge of the road. Abhi sang happily, 'A for apple!'

Swati braked swiftly.

'We're idiots!'

David and Mayukh were shocked by her outburst and then she burst out laughing.

'We're so used to getting food in boxes and packages that we've forgotten where it all comes from!'

She got out of the van and ran out towards the nearest tree, and Mayukh saw what she meant. He felt like kicking himself for not thinking of it earlier. They were driving by the edge of an apple orchard, and less than ten feet from them were several trees laden with fresh apples.

They got out and tried to get at the apples that hung tantalisingly close at hand. However, it soon became apparent that every branch within arm's reach had already been stripped bare. So they tried hoisting Abhi onto Mayukh's shoulders, at which he squealed in delight.

'See, I'm as tall as a giraffe!'

After what seemed to be an eternity, they found themselves laughing, especially when he quickly plucked two apples. But beyond that, everything else was out of reach. They divided the two apples between them, devouring them in minutes. Mayukh said he would try to climb one of the trees, when Abhi suddenly said aloud, 'That girl has apples for us.'

They turned and looked on astonished at a little girl, no more than six or seven years old, who stood just feet away, munching way at an apple with several more of the fruit lying in a basket that she had looped around her arm. She looked at them without a trace of fear, and then slipped into the thick forest behind her. Mayukh followed her, and after a second's thought, David and Swati followed him, Abhi holding onto Swati's hand.

Mayukh struggled to keep up with the girl as she meandered through the thick overgrowth. He kept calling out to her to wait, and that they meant no harm. Suddenly he found himself in a clearing and was soon joined by the others.

'Where did the girl go?'

Mayukh looked around but could see no sign of her. Tired, sleep-deprived and famished, he was panting from the short chase and went down on his haunches, trying to catch his breath.

'She seems to have disappeared. Anyway, that was a waste of time. Let's get back to the van.'

They had begun to turn back, when from the trees around them men rappelled down using ropes and surrounded them. The men were bare-chested and wearing tattered loincloths and carrying a combination of knives, axes and sticks. Mayukh was lifting his shotgun when David asked him to stop.

'Mayukh, there must be twenty of them. At such close quarters, we'll get one or two before they butcher us. Anyway, somehow, I don't think they mean to attack us.'

Mayukh took a closer look at the men around them. They all looked terrified, their eyes wide with panic and fear, and when he put his gun down, he could sense them relax. One of them, slightly taller and better built than the others, stepped forward, examining Mayukh and his friends. His gaze seemed to linger on Abhi, and then Mayukh could see the hint of a smile forming on his face. He looked at Abhi.

'Are you the one, little boy?'

Abhi looked up at the man, and said with defiance in his voice, 'I am three, not one. I am a big boy now.'

Despite the tension in the air, Mayukh, Swati and David couldn't help but smile and the man in front of Abhi also laughed out loud. The tension seemed to dissipate as the man whistled and his friends relaxed, lowering their weapons. A dozen or more women now appeared from within the trees, many with small children tied to their backs and others leading children by the hand. The girl they had seen on the road was there, still carrying her apples. The man who had spoken to Abhi motioned to the girl and she gave them an apple each, which they bit into gratefully. The man looked at some of the others standing behind him.

'Four of you stand watch.'

Then he sat down, and Mayukh and the others followed suit.

'My name is Ganesh. We were all workers in the orchards here before the ... problems started. The first night the demons came to our village and took many of us so those that remained hid in the orchards.'

'Ganesh, how have you stayed safe so long?'

The man seemed a bit surprised at how fluent David was in Hindi.

'We have all grown up in these orchards so we've hidden in the thicker parts of it which the demons don't know yet. They haven't yet gone so deep inside. When they do, we'll think of something else.'

Now that he mentioned it, Mayukh took a closer look at the trees and saw thatched areas on each tree, which almost looked like nests. He smiled in admiration at the ingenuity Ganesh and his friends had shown to survive so long.

'Uncle, can you swing from one tree to another like Tarzan?'

Ganesh looked at Abhi, puzzled since he had never heard of Tarzan, so Abhi tried a different tack.

'No, no, maybe like George of the jungle!'

Now, his stomach full with an apple in it, Abhi was back to full form as he began singing.

'George, George, George of the jungle, friend to you and me ...'

Swati was trying to hush him in vain as everyone smiled.

Ganesh's eyes suddenly turned serious. 'We heard about the ashram and that the boy was there.'

Mayukh was really curious about how everyone seemed to know about Abhi so he asked Ganesh.

'Everyone knows. At a time like this, any flicker of hope spreads like wildfire. One of our women supplied apples to the ashram in return for food supplies, and she heard about the boy who cannot be hurt by the demons.'

Two women brought forward a meal of rice and boiled potatoes and placed it in front of the four of them, ladling the food onto leaves. It was a simple meal, but as Mayukh put the hot rice in his mouth, he thought it was the most delicious meal he had ever had.

Swati spoke to one of the women serving them. 'Thank you. I know you must have limited food, so thank you for sharing it with us.'

The woman looked at Swati and gently tousled Abhi's hair.

'Daughter, I am an uneducated apple picker, and I don't know or understand many things, but in the midst of all this darkness, this boy is the only sign of hope we have.'

Ganesh touched Mayukh's arm gently, almost pleading with him. 'Keep him safe and see if he can help us remove this darkness that has fallen upon us.'

It was close to ten in the morning, and Mayukh heard from Ganesh that Ladakh was a good five-hour drive away.

He wanted to get going as soon as they could, but they were all dead tired and badly needed some rest and sleep. Ganesh and his friends spread out some blankets in the orchard and they lay down, asking to be woken up in a couple of hours. For the first time in many days, Mayukh slept peacefully, and when he was awakened by a gentle nudge from Swati, he woke with a smile on his face.

'Why are you smiling?'

Mayukh sat up and held her hand, trying to remember and savour every detail of his dream.

'I saw us—you, Abhi, me. Together. Walking into a mall, eating fast food, watching a movie, doing the small things we took for granted.'

Mayukh could see Swati's eyes get misty, when Abhi cut in.

'If we're having fast food, I want French fries.'

They laughed and got up to prepare for what they all hoped would be the last leg of their journey.

It was now just past one in the afternoon and they had driven for almost an hour through a landscape that saw the lush orchards of the Manali area give way to long stretches of barren rock, a forerunner of the desolate mountain passes they were headed towards. Swati was still driving, with Mayukh sitting in the back, playing the role of part babysitter and part gunner, with Abhi on his lap and his shotgun by his side. David was watching all the road signs and trying to ensure that they did not get lost in the hilly passes. Despite it being in the middle of the afternoon, the cold was already getting so severe that they stopped once to put on an extra layer of clothes, and eat more apples to give them some energy.

David noticed Swati's breath quicken as she seemed to be gasping for air, so he asked her to pull over.

'Swati, we're now at a much higher altitude than you may be used to, and the air will keep getting thinner. So the oxygen may not go to your brain as efficiently as it normally does. Don't panic, just take slow, deep breaths and you should be okay.'

When they started off again, Swati tried to heed his advice, but she found it tough going. Mayukh seemed to be coping much better with the altitude and they swapped places. There was no sign of anyone around, so they did not really think twice about not having the extra firepower of the shotgun readily available.

Abhi was in high spirits, boosted by the apples he had eaten. The adults—worried about what lay ahead and missing Hina's presence—were almost envious of his childish ability to live fully in the present. So he delighted in pointing out birds he saw, and screamed in delight when they saw what appeared to be a deer dashing into the trees. Despite the hilly terrain, Mayukh was trying to go as fast as he could, conscious of the fact that they needed to reach Ladkah before sunset.

David suddenly shouted in triumph.

'Just saw a sign. Ten kilometres more to Rohtang Pass. We're well on our way!'

Mayukh knew that was both good news and bad news. Good because they were making steady progress, bad because from what the guide had said, after Rohtang Pass, they would well and truly be in mountain terrain. The roads would not allow them to go as fast, and he was also increasingly worried about how Swati would cope with the altitude as they went higher.

After another half an hour of driving, they decided to stop for a break. Mayukh's arms and legs were cramped and aching from manoeuvring the sharp turns, and he was exhausted from paying such close attention to the road. David was of course not in any position to drive, and Swati bravely volunteered, but one glance at her told both Mayukh and David that she was in no shape to drive either. David handed each of them an apple.

'Eat and rest for ten, then we start again. We'll get through Rohtang in a few minutes, and then it should be no more than a couple of hours.'

Mayukh sat down on the ground, his back to the van, preparing for the home stretch. Swati came over and sat beside him, resting her head against his shoulder as he pulled her close.

'What are you thinking, Mayukh?.'

Mayukh held her hands and looked at her.

'Swati, I came so close to losing you at the ashram, and that terrified me. I was just wondering what is waiting for us up ahead.'

Swati smiled as she stroked his hair.

'Mayukh, no matter what's waiting for us, we will face it together. When it all started, I just wanted to run away and hide with Abhi somewhere and hope that things would get better. Now with all that has happened, we can't wait for things to get better. We have to make it happen, and if getting Abhi to Ladakh is what it takes, then I will do anything I can to make it happen.'

Abhi was busy playing with some rocks by the roadside, and when David tried to tell him it was time to go, he looked at him with his wide eyes.

'But I want to play!'

No amount of cajoling could get him to budge, so finally David decided he'd try another strategy.

'Come on and I'll tell you a story.'

That got Abhi's attention. 'What story is that?'

'Remember Mayukh told you about the boy who needed to be brave? This one's about how that boy met a brave and beautiful princess. Want to hear it?'

Abhi whooped in excitement and got into the van as David winked at Swati.

'Will the brave princess also get in?'

It was now four in the evening. Mayukh was beginning to wonder if their decision to take a nap in the morning would come back to haunt them. They passed a sign proclaiming they were beyond Rohtang Pass, and soon enough, a breath-taking vista of snow-capped mountains unfolded before them. There was not a soul in sight as they continued down the highway, which was in much better shape than any of them had imagined.

When David saw several abandoned army trucks by the roadside, he realised that the roads must have been kept in good condition to allow easy transport of soldiers and equipment to Ladakh, which he knew was a strategic choke point near both the Chinese and Pakistani borders.

They drove for another hour of what seemed to be bliss. It was as if they had come out for a picnic together, instead of having endured the horrors they had been subjected to over the last week. Abhi kept pointing to birds in the clear sky and at the snow in the mountains around them. It was the first time he had seen snow, and he cried out loud, 'Is that a giant ice-cream cone?'

Swati forgot about the troubles she was having breathing and Mayukh joined her in singing some old songs. They discovered that they both liked Ronan Keating and soon they were crooning away with a pretty off-key rendition of 'When You Say Nothing at All'. David, not one for pop, couldn't help but wince at their singing skills, but equally, he could not help but get caught up in everyone's excitement and enthusiasm either. Once they had finished singing, he treated them to his own rendition of 'Enter Sandman', which Mayukh assured him sounded nothing at all like the original.

And so they continued through the hilly roads, seeing nobody or nothing other than the occasional car or army truck by the roadside and making good progress. Then, as he saw a sign by the roadside, David struck a note of caution.

'Folks, we should probably be a bit more careful in the stretch ahead.'

'Why, what's up ahead?'

David turned to look at Swati to answer her question.

'We just passed some place called Keylang, and up ahead is Baralacha. The guide had said that the roads there suck.'

Mayukh laughed. 'Could our navigator be a bit more specific about how it sucks?'

David punched him playfully on the shoulder.

'It can be dangerous because there'll be frost around this time of the year, and the roads are narrow to begin with. Now can our fearless driver concentrate a bit more on driving instead of singing?'

Five minutes later, Mayukh's smile had vanished. If anything, the guide's warning had been an understatement. To his right, the valley was hundreds of feet below, while up ahead, he could see no more than a few feet before the road turned again. He thanked his stars that at least he didn't have to worry about traffic coming from the other direction, but with the bumpy, narrow and winding road, he was having more than his share of trouble in managing to keep them in one piece.

David's joking also stopped completely. He watched the road with great concentration, as did Swati, who was trying her best not to shout out warnings to Mayukh. She knew the last thing he would want at this time was backseat driving from her. Abhi, bored by what he saw as the sudden lack of interest from the adults, had curled up in Swati's lap and fallen asleep, happily oblivious to the bumps.

As Mayukh turned a corner, the van suddenly lurched and he struggled to keep it from veering off the cliff to his right. David leaned over and with his right hand helped Mayukh pull the steering wheel as Mayukh applied the brakes. The van came to a halt, one wheel almost at the edge of the cliff.

David got out of the van, hoping that it was not what

he feared it would be. He exclaimed loudly and let loose a stream of expletives.

'What's wrong?'

Mayukh got out and shouted in exasperation when he saw what David saw.

Two of their tyres were flat, and in the hurry to get away from the ashram, nobody had even checked if they had spares, and Swati soon confirmed that they didn't.

So some eight thousand feet above sea level, in the biting cold, with one hour or less to go before sunset, the four of them gathered together to face what the night was to bring.

TWELVE

'THEY'RE COMING.'

Abhi had spoken in no more than a mere whisper, but Mayukh, David and Swati stopped in their tracks. Mayukh put him down and knelt before him, looking into his eyes.

'Abhi, who is coming?'

Abhi pointed to a cluster of huts a few kilometres to their left.

'The not-nice people are coming.'

David took a good look in the direction Abhi was pointing and then turned towards the boy.

'Abhi, don't worry, I don't see anybody out there. I don't think they're coming.'

Abhi didn't look very convinced and muttered, barely audible to the others, 'But I can feel them coming.'

Swati had been trekking through the hilly terrain with the others, gamely trying to keep up and not slow the others down for the last hour since they had abandoned the van and proceeded on foot. The sun had just begun to set, and David had told them that based on what he remembered from the guide, they were still at least a couple of hours walk away from the Thirse Monastery. They had taken turns carrying Abhi through much of the journey, with Mayukh taking on the lion's share. Swati had volunteered to carry her brother when she had seen Mayukh tiring.

But she seemed to lose much of her composure at Abhi's words.

'What if they're really out there?'

Mayukh tried to sound confident, but was too tired to do a convincing job.

'Look, we haven't seen a soul for hours. The best we can do is to just keep walking. Come on, Swati. Hang in there, we're so close.'

David was watching their exchange, and suddenly he picked up the small bag filled with apples and water he had been carrying and started walking. Mayukh called after him.

'David, where are you going?'

He turned towards them, his face all business.

'After all we've been through to get so far, I'm not about to quit. If we do, all that pain, all that loss, Hina—all of it would have been for nothing. Now, are you coming or not?'

Swati said nothing, but picked up her own small bag and followed, and Mayukh picked Abhi on his back and was but a step behind.

It was practically pitch black, especially with no lights on in any of the nearby villages, and the cold was almost unbearable. They were all wearing gloves and caps and had bundled up Abhi as much as they could, but as Mayukh walked, he could feel the cold breeze bite into his face like a thousand needles. Swati cast anxious looks at Abhi, wondering if there was any truth to what he had said, but for now, Abhi seemed content to be riding on Mayukh's back.

They stopped for a short break, to have a bite to eat as

well as plan the last leg of their journey. Mayukh's relief at the break from walking with Abhi's weight on his back was matched only by Abhi's visible disappointment as he pouted, 'But I want to go piggyback again!'

Swati hushed him, bribing him with an apple that he began munching into immediately. David had siphoned off some fuel from the van and filled three bottles with it. Mayukh carried one of the Molotov cocktails, and David had the other two. Now, he and Mayukh broke off two sturdy branches from a nearby tree, tore one of their bags into two and fashioned crude torches from them. David had also taken a lighter from the van's glove compartment, and he poured some of the fuel on the torches and set them alight. They were instantly grateful both for the warmth and the fact that they were now no longer walking totally blind. David carried one and Swati the other, with Mayukh continuing to carry Abhi on his back and both shotguns slung over one shoulder.

As they proceeded, David whispered to Mayukh, 'I know we had to make the torches, but I have a bad feeling.'

'Why?'

'Because if anybody is actually out there looking for us, we're now practically lit up like a neon sign.'

Swati overheard him and spoke up, more hope than certainty in her voice, 'But if there is a government base out there, they'll also see us more easily.'

As soon as she said it, she clammed up, and none of them brought it up again. They had been proceeding so far on the leap of faith that there actually *was* a base where they could find safety. All they had to go on was that one radio broadcast, and if they were wrong, they would likely all die in this snow-covered wasteland.

Mayukh sensed what Swati was feeling and walked next to her, holding her hand. He wished he could have spent more time with her, wished he could have done all the things a young man would have done for the young woman in his life. But for now, all he could do was to hold her hand wordlessly as they continued trudging on the road frosted over with snow.

Mayukh could feel Abhi's head now resting against his back. The boy had no doubt fallen asleep and he wondered aloud how long it would take for them to get to their destination.

David looked at him and sighed. 'I'm not really sure. There aren't any road signs I can see ... at the rate we're going, it could be anything from thirty minutes to an hour more.'

Finally, they came upon a fork in the road with a small temple or pagoda drawn on a sign by the roadside. David remembered from the guide that they needed to keep going straight as the narrow path to their right supposedly led to a smaller monastery a few miles away. Seeing the sign gave them all renewed hope, since it meant that they were on the right track and not far from their destination.

They walked for a few more minutes when suddenly Mayukh felt a jerk as Abhi sat upright.

'They're coming.'

A nightmare, Mayukh thought, but nevertheless looked around for signs of movement. When he didn't see anything, he looked wordlessly towards Swati. The poor boy would be terrified and exhausted after all he had gone through. She tried to distract Abhi with a story, but he began crying and would not be consoled, and then David stopped.

He had not seen anything. In the dark with only their makeshift torches for light, he couldn't see beyond a few feet anyway, and he had not heard anything. But he had felt it. The same feeling he had experienced several times in combat, the instinct that had come from years of training that told him there was danger.

'David, you okay?'

David looked at him, and Mayukh saw that same inscrutable, stony gaze he had seen on the soldier's face when he had been in action before—in front of the bookstore, at the ashram. One evening, when he had mentioned it to David, he had jokingly called it his 'war face', but on a more serious note, had told him that it came when he was intensely focused on action, reacting with instinct and training.

Abhi once again insisted that *they* were coming, but more than the boy's insistence, David's expression scared Mayukh.

Swati could also sense the change in David's mood, and was about to ask him if he had heard anything, when they all heard it.

It was the sound of a mob on the move, the shuffling and stomping noises of many feet coming towards them. It was further amplified in the utter silence of the mountainous wasteland, and Swati felt her own pulse quicken.

'Could it be government soldiers?'

David shook his head. 'The sound is coming from behind us. Someone is following us.'

They were standing in the middle of the road, and suddenly they felt totally naked and exposed. David seemed to be thinking over something, and then as if making up his mind, sighed and turned to Mayukh.

'Mayukh, see that high snow bank there? Take Swati and Abhi and hide behind it. Swati, give me your torch so they don't see where you're heading.'

He tucked his own torch under his left armpit and took the other from Swati, who was not sure what he planned to do. Then it struck Mayukh.

'David, no! We're in this together.'

David looked at him, his eyes softening.

'Kid, you've been more than a brother these last few days. You're like family now, and as much as I'd like for all of us to make it together, what matters is that Abhi gets to safety. The only way any of this will be worth anything is if someone can figure out why he's immune to the Biters and help others. Now go.'

Swati was crying and Mayukh felt himself choke up as he said, 'I can't let you fight them alone. Remember what you said about the guy next to you?'

David turned to him, dead serious now.

'Mayukh, the fight's not over. You still need to get Abhi to the monastery. I'll just try and buy you some time.'

Then he turned towards Swati, touching her face gently.

'Take care of yourself and the two men in your life. And don't worry about me—I'm a hard guy to get rid of easily, and I do want to get back to Rose. Chances are you'll hear from me one day. If not, know I tried my best and tell my Rose about me.'

He handed her a small piece of paper with a name and a telephone number.

Then he was gone.

David walked back to the fork in the road and looked back once to ensure that Mayukh and the others were safely behind cover. In the darkness, it was hard to see much but he could barely make out the outline of the snow bank, and he could discern no movement. If his eyes, which were trained to operate in darkness, couldn't make them out, he had to bet on the fact that the Biters wouldn't figure out their plan either.

The thump-thump of the approaching Biters was now louder than ever, even though he couldn't see them yet. He knew there was a turn in the road, blocked by a small hill that they had passed minutes ago, and as the sound of approaching footsteps grew louder, he judged that they would be about to turn the bend any minute. The turn, bordered by a sheer cliff on one side and the hillside on the other, was such that even a very large mob would have to pass through two or three at a time.

He cocked back his right arm and threw the torch with all his strength. The torch spiralled into the sky, lighting up the ground below it like a flare and in its dull orange glow, David saw a sight that chilled him.

The first Biters had just emerged from the turning and behind them, he could see the pass packed with so many Biters it was hard to count them all. As the first Biters saw the other torch lit in David's hand, they bared their teeth and screamed, a cry that was taken up by the others till their unearthly howling filled the valley.

David ensured his pistol was tucked into his belt, and looked back once in the direction where Mayukh, Swati and Abhi were hiding.

Then he did the single most absurd thing he had ever done in his life. With one broken hand, two makeshift Molotov cocktails that he was not even sure would catch fire in the cold and frost, and a pistol that had only four rounds left in it, he turned towards the hundred or more Biters closing in on him. Then David charged towards them, screaming the battle cry of the US Navy SEALs.

'Hooyah!'

Mayukh heard David's yell, and as much as his heart cried out for him to go to his friend's assistance, he knew what he needed to do. He grabbed Swati by the hand, and with Abhi tied firmly to his back, he began running up the road as fast as he could. His ears were ringing with the screaming of the Biters, and when he looked back, he saw several fiery shapes flicker in the night before disappearing. He kept running, wanting to put as much distance as possible between them and the Biters. He could hear Swati gasping and panting, trying desperately to catch her breath, but he had her wrist in a vice-like grab and literally dragged her along.

He then heard four shots ring out in quick succession.

And then silence.

As he ran, tears streamed down his cheeks and he could tell from Swati's sobs that she was also crying. David was gone. With that stab of grief came a realisation. Now he was all that Swati and Abhi had.

For the next few minutes, the Biters seemed to be quiet, and all he heard were his own jagged breaths, Swati's panting, and the scraping of their shoes on the frosty road. Abhi was quiet and clinging to Mayukh's neck so tightly that he could feel the boy's nails bite into his skin. He could only guess how terrified Abhi must be.

Mayukh had not the foggiest idea how far the monastery was, but now was not the time to stop and check road signs. Doing that would mean using some form of light, even if it was only the lighter in Mayukh's pocket, and he didn't want to risk that. All he was focused on was going as fast as he could along the road they were on.

He suddenly felt Swati's hand jerk free of his, and he tried to hold on, grabbing a fistful of her jacket sleeve. Swati screamed loudly once, and then perhaps aware of the dangers noise could bring, did not say a word more, though Mayukh could hear her gasping. She seemed to have fallen, her weight dragging him down till he was on his knees. His eyes were now more accustomed to the dark, and in the moonlight, he could see that Swati seemed to be hanging from the edge of a cliff.

Mayukh cursed himself. He had been so focused on a headlong flight, he had not considered that the straight road they had been on might give way to more treacherous terrain. He grabbed her with both hands and inch by painful inch, pulled her up over the edge.

Now that Mayukh was sitting on the ground, he realised just how little he had left in him to carry on. All he wanted to do was to lie down, Biters or no Biters.

Abhi was crying, and Mayukh was too tired to tell him to be quiet.

Swati burrowed her head into his chest. 'Mayukh, I can't go any further. I can't even breathe properly. Just leave me here—'

She never got to finish as Mayukh kissed her.

'No, not you. Not you as well. I've lost too many people. I will not lose you.'

Abhi spoke up, his voice barely audible to Mayukh even though the boy's head was inches from Mayukh's ear.

'Don't be sad. I won't cry. I promise I'll be a brave boy.'

Swati hugged her brother and willed herself to carry on.

Mayukh had never felt as helpless and weak as this. His body was about to give up on him, and he had nothing left to offer Swati by way of reassurance.

'Swati, I'm sorry. I'm sorry I couldn't do more.'

She hugged both Mayukh and Abhi and her voice seemed composed. 'All that matters to me now is that we're together. No matter what happens, we will face it together. Now let's go!'

Abhi was smiling, happy that Mayukh and Swati were in better spirits. He was cold and scared, only too aware that the not-nice people were somewhere around. He wanted to reassure Mayukh, to make him feel happier, but his toddler's vocabulary wouldn't let him say much, so he remembered the story Mayukh had often told him.

'I'll be brave like the boy in the story. I'll remember what his daddy told him.'

Mayukh heard Abhi's words just a split second before he heard the thumping and shuffling of several feet behind them. Any doubts about who they might be were dispelled when he began to hear their screams.

'Jiiiiiiihaaaaaaaaaaaaaad.'

'The boy give us.'

The number of footsteps seemed fewer than before, so either David had thinned their ranks, or only some of them had taken this road. Or perhaps only some of them had heard Swati's screams. Mayukh knew that no matter how many of the Biters were there, it was now too late to run.

Abhi's words triggered the memory of what his own father had told him. Indeed, what had been his last words to Mayukh.

Be the man I always dreamed you would be.

A clarity came over Mayukh, and he somehow felt physically lighter, as if a burden had been lifted from him. He began to untie Abhi from his back.

'Mayukh, what are you doing?'

Mayukh ignored Swati as he tied Abhi to Swati's chest, the boy facing her. Then he held Swati with both hands.

'I know you're tired. I know it hurts, and I know he's heavy for you. But you must go on. You must make it.'

She was now crying. 'I can't leave you. I love you!'

Mayukh felt his own eyes well up.

'I love you too. More than I can tell you now. But that's why you need to go. That's why Hina and David did what they did for us. Whatever happens, Abhi must make it.'

He kissed Abhi on the forehead once, and then kissed Swati hard, lingering to feel her one last time. Then he dragged her to her feet and pushed her to get her started on her way. She was crying, but began to resolutely run down the road.

He kept looking in her direction till the sound of her footsteps faded. Then Mayukh turned to face the Biters.

Mayukh was surprised to find that he felt no fear. His mind was more at peace than he ever remembered. As he heard the thumps and scrapes of the Biters' approaching footsteps get louder and closer, he thought back to all he had been through. Seventeen years of indulgence and not taking anything seriously, of throwing tantrums over what now seemed to be trifles; and then in seven days, experiencing life more intensely than in all those preceding years combined. He had found love, learnt the meaning of responsibility, learnt what it was to sacrifice for others, learnt what true friendship meant, and above all else, learnt how good it felt to live for someone else for a change. The howls of the mob of Biters seemed ever closer, and he thought he heard a voice whisper in his head. He could have sworn it was David.

You've learnt to be a man, soldier.

Mayukh smiled and took out his iPhone from his pocket. It showed the battery to be thirty per cent charged, which was far more than he figured he'd need. He tapped on the Flashlight app. He had downloaded it for fun some months ago, and not used it once after the first day of fiddling with it. The app was on Strobe Mode, casting a brilliant blue and white glow around the phone. The Biters must have noticed the glow for they screamed louder than ever and he could hear the sound of running feet.

He knelt and skipped his phone along the road, thinking that, even if it broke, he had no use for it anymore, just praying that it stayed screen up. The phone bounced off the road and came to a halt a dozen or so feet away, lighting up its surrounding area like a small beacon. Mayukh could see the first of the Biters now, a gnarled, deformed face with a turban tied on top. The Biter seemed to be dressed in the torn remains of what seemed to be a police uniform of some sort. Three more dressed like him were just behind.

Mayukh took the Molotov cocktails and lit the bit of cloth extending out of its top with his lighter. He fumbled once or twice, and realised that in the cold, the fuse was not catching fire as he had hoped it would. The first Biter was less than six feet away when Mayukh put the lighter to the neck of the plastic bottle itself. He felt a flash of searing heat for a second before he flung the bottle at the Biter.

The flaming bottle hit the Biter in the chest and he screamed as he fell. One of those behind him tripped over him and was also engulfed in the flames.

By the light of the fire, Mayukh now saw what he was up against. There were about two dozen Biters rushing towards him. The good news was that meant David had either distracted or killed a huge number of the original pursuing force. The bad news was that at such close quarters, even a dozen Biters were a dozen too many.

Mayukh unslung a shotgun and pumped it, chambering a round and firing, seeing one Biter, a ghoul who looked like he had been a chef, still dressed in his white uniform, get cut in two. He swivelled towards the next one, and realised this Biter was no more than a boy, perhaps seven or eight years old, and wearing a Mickey Mouse t-shirt. Or rather, he *had* been a boy, Mayukh corrected himself as he pulled the trigger. He fired three more times, not aiming at anyone in particular, but sure that at such close range, he couldn't miss.

Then the first of the Biters reached him—one who had been an elderly woman, with wisps of grey hair still sticking out from under her turban, her face a yellowy, bloody mess that was barely visible in the light that the pyres of the two burning Biters were still throwing up.

Mayukh reversed his shotgun slammed the butt into her head, and as she rocked back, he turned it around and fired, all but obliterating her. He fired twice more before his shotgun ran out of shells. A strong hand gripped his right arm and another ripped the shotgun from his hands. He kicked out, and felt his leg connect with something, but then another hand reached out and grabbed his foot in a vice-like grip.

Mayukh went down on one knee, as a Biter jumped on his chest. Mayukh was thrown back, the wind totally knocked out of him. Flat on his back, he could only see the outline of the Biter's head, but he could smell its fetid odour, a foul, reeking stench that made him gag almost involuntarily. The Biter was now closing in on Mayukh, its open mouth seeking his neck.

Mayukh fished in his pocket with his free left hand and took out the lighter, bringing it up between him and the Biter before flicking it on. He caught a glimpse of a yellowed, deformed face with a beard before the Biter shrieked and fell off him, fire enveloping his beard.

Mayukh tried to get back on his feet but a blow to his head sent him down again. He could feel blood flowing down the side of his head, and wondered if a Biter had hit him with a rock. He tried to reach for the second shotgun slung on his left shoulder but a kick sent pain wracking through his body, as he heard his ribs crack.

He felt arms grab his hands, and then his feet, till he could no longer move.

The Biters were now screaming again, excited at the kill, and Mayukh thought that perhaps it was just as good that he had pissed them off as much as he had. He knew that they tore apart those who fought them, but that was a fate far better than being bitten and transformed into one of them.

He saw a Biter move in for the kill, its sharp teeth bared, ready to tear Mayukh's throat out before the others cut him to ribbons. Mayukh rocked his head forward, catching the Biter completely by surprise by smashing his head into its face. Mayukh felt a rush of pain, and then a free flow of blood down his face. He was sure he had broken his nose, but he was not done fighting yet. It wasn't about saving his own life—he had already reconciled to being a dead man. It was the simple fact that every minute he delayed the Biters was an extra minute that Swati and Abhi had to get to safety.

As the Biter above him growled in fury and brought his mouth down to bite him, Mayukh smashed his head into the Biter again. Mayukh didn't know if the Biters felt pain or not, but this one was at least knocked off balance enough to be thrown off Mayukh. As for Mayukh, if he had not broken his nose the first time, this time around he was sure he had succeeded.

Infuriated by this unexpected resistance, another Biter picked up a rock and hit Mayukh with it. Mayukh saw the blow coming and held his right hand up in front of his face, taking the full strength of the blow on his elbow. He screamed in agony, sure that some bones had broken where the rock had connected. When his right hand dropped uselessly to his side, the Biter brought up the rock for another blow. In the melee, the grip on his right leg had loosened, and Mayukh kicked out at where he judged the Biter's groin to be. He connected with something soft, but the Biter didn't seem to notice.

Armed with the useless bit of trivia that Biters were not fazed by a kick to their balls, Mayukh felt the rock connect with his head. As his head flopped back on the cold road, a deep sigh escaped from Mayukh's lips. He had done the very best he could. Now he had no more fight left in him.

Bruised, bloodied and battered, Mayukh looked up at the stars in the sky, hoping that the end would not be too painful, and praying that he had bought Swati and Abhi enough time.

As he saw the Biters' silhouettes loom over him, he thought he saw shooting stars crisscrossing the sky, and then the sound of firecrackers bursting. Whatever it was, he had neither the curiosity nor the energy to find out; perhaps it was some Biter with a gun.

He felt cold, clammy hands close around his neck, and he shut his eyes. His last thought was that perhaps it was good that he was going to be unconscious when the Biters tore into him.

THIRTEEN

'YOU LOOK like the mummy!'

Mayukh would have smiled had it not hurt so much to move his face. He would have loved to hug Abhi and Swati back when they clutched him, but his right hand was in a cast. He would have loved to hold Swati much longer, but his ribs hurt when she rested against him. In short, he could do very little to show them just how deliriously happy he was to see them again, so he did the one thing his body still allowed him to do.

He cried.

Two medics walked in and changed the IV drips that were attached to him, and then a man in an Indian army uniform walked in. He looked to be at least fifty from the grey in his hair, but his posture was still ramrod straight and Mayukh saw that he was supremely fit. He seemed as if about to extend a hand to shake Mayukh's, and then a bit sheepishly, took his hand back.

'You, sir, have had quite an adventure.'

To Mayukh, that was the understatement of the century.

The man introduced himself as Major General Vij and sat down next to Mayukh.

'How long have I been here?'

He could see Swati smile as the general answered.

'You've been out for almost three days.'

Three days!

Mayukh turned to Swati and Abhi as if seeking answers as to what had happened. Trying to find out how he had been rescued when he was sure he was going to die at the hands of the Biters. Trying, above all, to find out if getting Abhi all the way to Ladakh had actually helped in any way whatsoever.

Swati was still holding onto his left hand as if afraid to let go, and Abhi was sitting on his lap as he sat propped up on the bed. Swati's eyes looked dead tired and bloodshot, and she seemed to be on the verge of falling asleep.

Before she could say anything, the general interrupted.

'Young man, she has been sitting by your side almost every minute of these three days, so she could do with some rest. You yourself still need some patching up and the doctors have said they may need to put you under general anaesthesia again. So just lie down, try and get some soup inside you—you haven't had any nutrition other than what was pumped in through the IV drips. Once she's rested and the doctor's finished with you, we'll talk. We all have a lot of catching up to do.'

Mayukh tried to protest, but his eyes seemed to be shutting of their own accord, and he dropped back onto the pillows behind him. Swati came close and kissed him on the cheeks once, whispering to him, 'Rest, my love. Now that you're back with me, I won't let you go anywhere. Just rest, and then we will talk.'

Abhi was giggling. 'She kissed him!'

Mayukh smiled and then winced in pain as some of the many stitches he now knew crisscrossed his face stretched. He watched Swati and Abhi leave the room with the general, and realised that no matter what else was to happen, it was worth it to see them safe.

There was so much he wanted to know. What had happened in the world outside? How many other safe zones like this one were there? And most of all, was there hope that they could rid the world of the Biters after all?

The door opened again and a young soldier came in, dressed in battle fatigues. From his sharp features, Mayukh guessed he was a Gurkha. The soldier pushed a table next to the bed and placed a bowl of steaming soup on it.

'Drink this. It tastes like shit but will give you strength.'

Mayukh looked at him, wondering how he was expected to drink the soup with a drip attached to his left hand and his right hand in a cast. The Gurkha produced a straw and put it in the bowl. He held the straw in place while Mayukh bent over and drank it.

The soup was hot, watery, tasted of frozen vegetables and preservatives, had way too much salt in it, and all things considered, was the most delicious meal Mayukh had eaten in the last ten days. He slurped it shamelessly and then fell back on his bed, tired even from the exertion of drinking. The Gurkha patted him on his left shoulder.

'By the way, did you really head-butt a Biter and kick another in the balls?'

Mayukh wondered how he knew, but his expression must have told the Gurkha what he needed to know, because he grinned and said, 'Get well soon. There are many soldiers here who want to hear your story, and buy you a drink.'

As soon as the Gurkha left, another soldier came in, though this time he was wearing a stethoscope around his neck and to Mayukh's surprise, was American. He smiled at Mayukh, checked the clipboard in his hands, and said, 'So, Mayukh, I'll give you some morphine for the pain and then we'll put you under anaesthesia. We still need to finish the stitches on the back of your head and I think today's when we try and reset your nose.'

Mayukh was going to ask about his injuries, but realised he didn't really want to know just how messed up he was. He sat back as the doctor gave him one injection in his left arm, and another in his hip. He grimaced a bit, but in a few seconds, he felt light-headed.

'Just close your eyes and lie down.'

Mayukh did that, and soon he was fast asleep.

It was a utilitarian room, stark metal grey with long benches and metal chairs. The food before them was the soup Mayukh had earlier and what looked like instant noodles. He had Swati sitting next to him, Abhi on her lap, and her fingers intertwined in his. Mayukh still hurt in a dozen places, and had been amazed he was alive when the full extent of his injuries was revealed to him. Three cracked ribs, a fractured hand, a broken nose, and nineteen stitches on his head and face. When he first looked at himself in the mirror, he had nearly jumped in fright at the heavily-bandaged apparition that stared back. The American doctor had been laconic about it.

'Wounds heal, and chicks dig scars.'

The room was filled with soldiers in uniform, a mix of

Indian and American faces, including several women, and Mayukh saw General Vij standing in a corner, dressed in what seemed to be his full dress uniform, with medals and ribbons across his chest and stars on his shoulders. Next to him was a middle-aged American soldier, dressed in a blue uniform with similar stars on his shoulders.

'Ladies and gentlemen, welcome to our briefing. Finish your soup and we will begin.'

That morning, Mayukh had been allowed visitors, and he had spent the whole day revelling in Swati's company. With Abhi awake, it was tough to do anything more than keep him entertained, but when he had taken a nap in the afternoon, Mayukh had finally gotten around to doing what he'd wanted to do ever since he had woken up.

He kissed Swati and told her that he loved her.

He had learnt a bit of what had happened here. American and Indian troops had been doing joint mountain warfare exercises when the first trouble broke out in Afghanistan. As things got worse, Vij and his American counterpart locked down the base and secured the Ladakh airfield. Over the next few days, more soldiers flew in seeking safety, and now there were more than ten thousand troops in the base and the airfield, about two thousand of them Americans.

That night in the mountains, Swati had bumped into an advance recon team, and they had followed her back to where Mayukh was trying to hold off the Biters. They had killed the Biters with their high-powered sniper rifles.

General Vij now spoke up again.

'This will be our first briefing in three days. As you know, since our latest guests arrived, we have been rather busy.'

Almost every pair of eyes in the room turned towards Mayukh and Swati, and when Mayukh looked back at several of them, he saw only welcoming smiles on the soldiers' faces.

The Indian general continued. 'Over the last three nights, we've faced no less than sixteen waves of assaults by the Biters.'

One of the soldiers put up his hand.

'How did we do, sir?'

Vij smiled.

'I don't have sharp teeth, yellow skin, do not wear a black turban and am not trying to bite you. So in summary, we survived.'

Many in the room chuckled, and Mayukh found himself liking the general's easy-going manner.

'We estimate more than three hundred Biters killed—with no losses on our side. They've never attacked us after the first day we set up here, and the fact that they came back shows how desperate they were to get to our guests.'

He paused to drink from a glass before continuing.

'I know the last couple of weeks have been tough. We all left friends and families back home, and I know how difficult it has been for each and every one of you to stay here and do your duty as well as you have. But the tide is turning. Let me share some updates from the outside world.'

Everyone seemed to sit up at that, and one of the soldiers near Mayukh whispered that they'd had no news from the outside for several days.

'First, the Indian prime minister is alive and well, and is currently on board the aircraft carrier INS *Viraat*, where the Government of India is currently based.'

Many of the Indian soldiers present cheered.

'They have established radio contact with us, and with the other Indian armed forces units like us still surviving.'

There was a palpable buzz of excitement. Mayukh guessed many of the soldiers must have wondered if there were others like them.

'The government has declared a state of war, and while we have been holding out for so long, now we are ordered to take the fight to the enemy. As of tomorrow, we will start coordinating with other units in commencing offensive operations against the Biters.'

Several cheers began echoing through the room as the general continued.

'And this time we will not have to fight the sons of bitches with our rifles and, in some cases, our heads alone.'

He glanced at Mayukh and smiled broadly—and many of the soldiers cheered and clapped.

'Air strikes from the INS *Viraat* and at least four airbases which are still in our hands are beginning, and paradrops are taking place today to occupy and sanitise other airbases so we can bring more air power to bear. Now I'll hand over the briefing to General Edwards.'

The American general took up where Vij had left off.

'Some good news for the Americans here as well. The president is well, and like the Indian prime minister, on an aircraft carrier. The same goes for the British, French and Russian leaders. The good news is that the bulk of our strategic arsenal—our naval assets, strategic missile forces, and long-range aviation assets—are all intact. Together, we are declaring war on these monsters and will reclaim our world. Our first coordinated move is to restore control over gas and electricity, so that we can restore those essentials to humans stranded in enemy-held territory. This includes communications as well.'

More cheers as he continued, with a more sombre tone.

'As you have heard and have seen, the Biters are learning—either evolving or accessing memories. So we've faced Biters with guns and in their last waves, one or two actually fired RPGs at us. Well, the bad news is that in what was Pakistan, we now know some Biters tried to activate their nuclear assets.'

Mayukh could feel the tension in the room as Edwards continued.

'To avoid an escalation and given the real possibility of Biters launching nuclear weapons against human targets, in consultation with surviving world leaders, the US president ordered tactical nuclear strikes against all known nuclear weapons locations in Pakistan.'

He paused as that sank in, and Mayukh heard more than one gasp, as the severity of that decision sank in. He looked around and saw that most of the soldiers had not even touched the food placed in front of them. Swati was gripping his hand tight.

Edwards continued. 'We will all meet later for detailed orders and deployments for upcoming combat operations, but thank you for all you have done.'

Vij now looked straight at Mayukh.

'Can I request our guests to come up and join me?'

As he walked up with Swati and Abhi, Mayukh felt really awkward, having hundreds of eyes focused on him. He passed the Gurkha who had served him food, and he smiled. The Gurkha saluted and started clapping. The entire room erupted then in thunderous applause as the three of them walked to join the generals. Edwards shook their hands and patted Abhi on the head, while Vij gently nudged Mayukh to the front.

'First of all, I wanted all of you to see these remarkable young people. You have all heard their story in one form or the other, but what they have achieved is amazing. When we put out our radio broadcast, we were hoping to attract people from nearby areas—and we did get several thousand, who are now at the airfield. But they made it all the way from Delhi, with all the adventures you have heard about.'

He glanced at Mayukh.

'You don't know this, but while the internet is still not up, the ham radio operators are as active as any chat forum, and for the last few days, all they have been chattering about is your adventure.'

Mayukh flushed a bit at all this unwanted attention. He certainly didn't want any attention, nor did he feel particularly brave. Everything he'd done was for the people with him, and without Hina or David to share the moment with them, it all seemed somewhat empty. Vij must have sensed what was on his mind, and spoke again for all those assembled in the room.

'More than anything else, you have all heard tales of this boy, who was not infected.'

Abhi was now holding onto Mayukh's left leg, looking more than a little intimidated at all the attention. When Vij turned to him and smiled, he pushed his face into Mayukh's leg.

'I must be honest: I had my doubts to begin with. Perhaps it was all an urban legend. Perhaps people were just trying to grasp at straws. But after having seen this little boy with my own eyes, it's obvious he was bitten from the wound and teeth marks on his leg, but was not transformed. When we sent out the message that we had him, a chopper from a US aircraft carrier came to pick up samples for testing at the American base at Diego.'

The following morning, Mayukh was sitting in the small room he was sharing with Swati and Abhi.

'What now?'

Those two words were simple enough for Swati to ask, but Mayukh didn't know how to answer. Their ordeal may have been over, but it was obvious the world was still very much at war, and that war was only going to get uglier as the human forces now organised themselves and retaliated against the Biters. There was no question of going back to any of the big cities, which had been the worst hit by the Biters epidemic, so he really didn't know what lay ahead for Swati and him. As he thought that, he corrected himself. No, he did know what lay ahead. He had been thinking in terms of where they may live, what they may do with their lives, but not about what they would do with each other. And if there was one thing he took away from the ordeal they had shared, that was all that really mattered.

'Swati, we've known each other for about two weeks, and we're both not yet out of school. So this may sound crazy, but maybe in a world gone crazy, this is the only thing that makes sense. I think the only thing I know with certainty is that you and I and Abhi are going to be together forever.'

She just smiled and whispered, 'Yes.'

He brought her closer to him and Abhi spoke up.

'Once you finish kissing, can you talk about cars with me?'

Mayukh picked up the boy and the three of them hugged, laughing together.

There was a gentle knock on the door. It was General Edwards.

'Son, they finished the tests from Abhi's blood samples. The reports will be with us any minute. I thought you'd want to be there.'

They were about to file out the door when Mayukh asked him if they had any news about David. The previous evening, he had related the full story of their trip and of the role David had played in it.

'Thanks to your detailed debriefing, we've already sent out search parties for Captain Bremsak. We recovered more than eight burnt Biter corpses where he made his stand, and then the trail indicates he jumped off the cliff, taking at least a few more with him.'

'Sir, is he ...'

The general caught his gaze as Mayukh saw a pin on the general's coat. An eagle perched on an anchor, holding a trident in its talons. He remembered seeing a similar pin on David.

'We don't know, son, but we will find him. We SEALs don't leave our own behind.'

EPILOGUE

MAYUKH AND SWATI beamed as they exchanged rings. They planned on getting married one day, but the engagement was an important step towards that. They were surrounded by laughter and cheers, but those came not from relatives, but from soldiers in combat fatigues at the US Air Force Base at Anchorage in Alaska.

They had flown there a month ago when Abhi's test results had come in, and it had been their home ever since. They had begun their life together, while the war still raged outside. The Biters could now operate tanks and heavy armour, and while the human forces had most of the air power, the brutal war continued.

Electricity had been restored in several places, and TV was back on—if a handful of news channels and a few entertainment channels showing reruns of old shows counted. They could have just hunkered down for a comfortable life at the base, but after all they had been through, they wanted to do more.

Being one of the few to have gotten so close to the Biters and lived to tell the tale, Swati and Mayukh began to help in briefing new recruits and also passing on survival tips to human communities everywhere. There were hundreds of millions spread around the world, living in cities where the Biters came out at night, or hiding in isolated farmlands, too scared to come out. They used the radio on the base to pass on tips and talk to them, and their story gave hope and their knowledge helped them survive till human forces got to them.

When he started out, Mayukh tried to get some information about what had happened to his father. He did get in contact with some government officials who had survived by going into hiding, but there was no news of his father. Mayukh's one regret was that his parents never got a chance to see what he had become, and the responsibilities he had shown himself capable of bearing.

But of all of them, the one who helped the most was Abhi. The doctors had already cloned vaccines from his blood samples, and these had been tested, showing that any human injected with it was resistant to being converted on being bitten. The doctors had their theories as to why Abhi was resistant- perhaps it was a gene mutation, perhaps he had been exposed to some toxins as a child; but the truth was that they had no real idea. But what was much more important than the reason for his immunity was the impact it had in the struggle against the Biters.

Old drug factories were quickly reclaimed by Special Forces and the vaccine was being churned out in the millions, to be distributed to human survivors everywhere. If they could get the vaccine to every human out there, one thing was certain. No more Biters would be created.

It was perhaps only appropriate that the solution to the madness and destruction the world had inflicted upon itself lay in the blood of an innocent child.

When Mayukh went in for his shift in the radio room later that day, one of the operators called him over. 'Mayukh, there's someone on the radio who wants to talk to you.'

Mayukh put on the headset and was electrified at the voice he heard.

'Congratulations, kid. Sorry I couldn't be there in person.'

Mayukh sputtered in astonishment.

'David! God, where are you? What happened to you?'

'Long story. I woke up in a farmer's hut, half dead and more than half frozen. Took them two weeks to get me coherent enough to tell them who I was. But my buddies didn't leave me. Of all the people I could have imagined meeting, once my story was out, I was picked up by two SEALs who took me to the base in Ladakh. By then, you were in Alaska and I thought I'd get home before I checked on you.'

'Did you find Rose?'

There was a brief silence on the other end.

'Kid, I found her. I buried her behind our old home.'

'Oh god, I'm so sorry, David.'

He could hear David sigh at the other end. 'No, Mayukh. It's better than never knowing. I buried her and then rejoined my unit. Hey, I gotta go now. I promise to come and visit you guys.'

'Where are you going?'

'The only place a SEAL can be at a time like this.'

David paused for a second before finishing.

'I'll be out hunting in Zombiestan.'

Mainak Dhar is a cubicle-dweller by day and author by night. He has written thirteen books, some of which are bestsellers as ebooks. Learn more about him and his writing at mainakdhar.com